Morpheus Tales: The Best Weird Fiction Volume

Edited By A

Morpheus Tales: The Best Weird Fiction Volume 1

Edited By Adam Bradley

Fiction By

Lyn Cannaday
Robert T. Canipe
Steven Lee Climer
Nickolas Cook
Garon Cockrell
Nick Day
Vic Fortezza
Ken Goldman
Gary Hewitt
Todd Austin Hunt
Michael Laimo
Kevin Lucia
Adrian Ludens
Christian McPhate
Mari Mitchell
Theresa C. Newbill
Aaron A. Polson
Jonathan J. Schlosser
Tommy B. Smith
Alan Spencer
Wayne Summers
Randy Young
Mark Zirbel
Lee Clark Zumpe

ISBN: 978-1-4710-7392-2

Cover By Matthew Freyer - http://www.matthewfreyerproductions.com

First edition, February 2012.

"Under The Bridge" copyright © 2008 By Wayne Summers
"Pristine" copyright © 2008 By Vic Fortezza
"He Said Something" copyright © 2008 By Todd Austin Hunt
"The Sliding" copyright © 2008 By Kevin Lucia
"The Darkest Of Waters" copyright © 2008 By Tommy B. Smith
"A Most Unfortunate Gaffe" copyright © 2008 By Aaron A. Polson
"Didn't Remind Me" copyright © 2008 By Robert T. Canipe
"Paper Wasp And Chocolate Rabbits" copyright © 2008 By Mari Mitchell
"Cicadas" copyright © 2008 By Nickolas Cook
"Bloody Kisses: Tragedy" copyright © 2008 By Christian McPhate
"All Pink On The Inside" copyright © 2008 By Steven Lee Climer
"Produce By" copyright © 2009 Gary Hewitt
"Alone in the Cataloochee Valley" copyright © 2009 By Lee Clark Zumpe
"Execution Day" copyright © 2009 By Alan Spencer
"Snow like lonely ghosts…" copyright © 2009 By Nick Day
"Being God" copyright © 2009 By Jonathan J. Schlosser
"And If Thine Eye Offend Thee" copyright © 2009 By Ken Goldman
"Off The Hook" copyright © 2009 By Michael Laimo
"Vampires Suck" copyright © 2009 By Lyn Cannaday
"Under The Placenta Tree" copyright © 2009 By Mark Zirbel
"Bloody Kisses: Blood Rose" copyright © 2009 By Christian McPhate
"Soap Sally" copyright © 2009 By Randy Young
"Prelude" copyright © 2009 By Garon Cockrell
"The Salty Skeleton" copyright © 2009 By Theresa C. Newbill
"A Story About Monsters" copyright © 2009 By Adrian Ludens
"Epitaph For Sol" copyright © 2009 By Tommy B. Smith

All rights reserved. No part of this publication may be reproduced, stored, or transmitted in any form, or by any means, including electronic, mechanical, photocopying, recording, or otherwise, without prior written permission of the copyright owners.

Works reprinted with the permission of the authors.

The right of the author to be identified as the author of this works has been asserted in accordance with the Copyright, Designs and Patents Act, 1988.

All characters in this publication are fictional and any resemblances to persons real, living or dead, is entirely coincidental.

Table of Contents

Introduction 1
Under The Bridge By Wayne Summers 3
Pristine By Vic Fortezza 11
He Said Something By Todd Austin Hunt 17
The Sliding By Kevin Lucia 22
The Darkest Of Waters By Tommy B. Smith 30
A Most Unfortunate Gaffe By Aaron A. Polson 37
Didn't Remind Me By Robert T. Canipe 43
Paper Wasp And Chocolate Rabbits By Mari Mitchell 48
Cicadas By Nickolas Cook 55
Bloody Kisses: Tragedy By Christian McPhate 64
All Pink On The Inside By Steven Lee Climer 69
Produce By Gary Hewitt 76
Alone in the Cataloochee Valley By Lee Clark Zumpe 82
Execution Day By Alan Spencer 89
Snow like lonely ghosts… By Nick Day 95
Being God By Jonathan J. Schlosser 100
And If Thine Eye Offend Thee By Ken Goldman 107
Off The Hook By Michael Laimo 112
Vampires Suck By Lyn Cannaday 120
Under The Placenta Tree By Mark Zirbel 125
Bloody Kisses: Blood Rose By Christian McPhate 130
Soap Sally By Randy Young 134
Prelude By Garon Cockrell 138
The Salty Skeleton By Theresa C. Newbill 146
A Story About Monsters By Adrian Ludens 149
Epitaph For Sol By Tommy B. Smith 152

Introduction

I love books. Books are permanent. Don't get me wrong, I love magazines too. But they tend to get thrown away, unless you're an avid collector. I have a collection of magazines and books, much to my girlfriend's delight!

When I started Morpheus Tales with a couple of friends back in 2008, we were on the verge of recession, the credit crunch was hitting, but I wanted to do it again. I wanted to be part of something. I wanted to edit a magazine.

Back in the mid-nineties I first got the bug. I visited my favourite bookshop (Forbidden Planet) every week, joined the British Fantasy Society and discovered the small press. My hunger was insatiable. As a poor student most of my money went on subscriptions rather than beer and beans. I was hooked. I wanted to be a part of this. I needed it.

Using a borrowed photocopier and PC, back in the days when the internet was just a myth, I started Black Tears Magazine. Meant as a one-off it became a quarterly magazine as the submissions (hard copies!) flooded in.

Two years after Black Tears started, Violent Spectres made an appearance. Darker, edgier with no non-fiction, Violent Spectres had an actual budget!

Another year in and Violent Spectres and Black Tears (my humble publishing empire!) were forced to close. Reality and paying bills overtook my love of fiction.

Ten years later I wanted to do it all over again.

The internet had changed the way publishing worked. Laser printers meant you could print high-quality copies, along with print-on-demand and ebook publishing.

Morpheus Tales began in 2008 as a quarterly magazine featuring SF, horror and fantasy fiction and non-fiction. By issue 7 the non-fiction section was too big to contain within the printed magazine and we launched the MT Supplement, a free online magazine. We brought in new blood, the team continued to grow, Tommy B. Smith provided the Dark Sorcery Special and the Urban

Horror Special. Trevor Wright worked on the Scream Queens trilogy.

We were developing a small-press. A real little publishing company. What should we do next? I asked my fellow founders. A book, someone stated, with such determination that grins spread across our faces and our eyes lit up.

Those first few issues of the magazine were more broad-based genre fiction as the magazine, and I, found ourselves. Later issues became more focused, the fiction became darker. Many issues are now out of print, available only through lulu.com as large format Collector's Editions. But these are good issues, these are the foundations on which Morpheus Tales is built. So, what better way to celebrate these first steps into publishing again, than by producing a best-of collection.

Although inspired by the genre-blending roots, the best-of collection shows the darker side of Morpheus Tales. The creepy, the chilling, the menacing and maniacal side. "Weird fiction" it says on the cover.

So follow us:
www.twitter.com/morpheustales

Befriend us:
www.myspace.com/morpheustales

www.facebook.com/morpheustales

And visit us (www.morpheustales.com) for more previews, free magazines and loads more!

Thanks for your support, and most of all, thanks for reading.

Welcome to the dark side of Morpheus Tales.

Adam Bradley

Under The Bridge By Wayne Summers

I remember Grandma Reilly standing at the wooden table in her kitchen in one of her floral, cotton dresses, beating eggs in a bowl tucked under one flabby arm, and telling us about the troll that lived under the bridge by the road. I'd listen with my eyes wide, under a long, dark brown fringe and a quickening thumping in my chest, and then when she'd finished I'd say, "But Grandma, that's not true, is it?". She'd reply that if I didn't believe her I could always go and ask Grandpa, only Grandpa was dead. There was always a twinkle in her eye as she said it and I never knew why until much later.

"What does the troll look like?" I used to ask, wanting to hear the grisliest details.

"Ooooh," Grandma Reilly would begin dramatically. "It looks like your worst nightmare."

And at that point she'd look directly at me, the biscuit in my hand poised in mid-air between the plate and my mouth.

"He's tall and skinny, with scaly green skin, covered in patches of thick, coarse hair. His eyes are yellow and bulging, and he's got thick, bright red lips, rubbed raw from eating so many children. Behind those big lips hide jagged, yellowing teeth, and breath so foul it could stop a charging elephant."

I'd then attempt a bit of my homemade biscuit, bringing it to the edge of my mouth, thinking that Grandma Reilly's description had ended, but it hadn't. Every time she told the story she would add to it.

"All hair and skin and bones it is," she'd continue, her breathing becoming shorter and more rapid as she whipped those eggs into a frothy lather. "Looks like it wouldn't eat much, but my word it does! You know it ate your grandpa, swallowed him whole and used his thigh bone to pick its teeth clean."

I'd look anxiously across at the door to check that the latch was in place and imagine that I could see the shadow of the troll in the space beneath the door.

"But Grandpa died in the war," I'd say, and Grandma Reilly would stop beating the eggs for a moment and peer over her specs at me.

"I know that's what they say, Pet," she'd reply mysteriously, "but that's because the truth is too scary for words. I, myself, won't go near that bridge, nor that part of the river! I don't mind taking the other bridge even if it adds another ten minutes to my journey. I know all too well what lies beneath the first one."

I can never forget how she'd glance at the door at that point, pretending to do it secretly, although always making sure I'd catch her. My grandma was so very crafty that I never knew for certain what was real and was not in these tales she would weave. The story of the troll terrified me the most since she herself seemed frightened.

One season followed another into the unending future. Grandma Reilly grew older and I grew into a man. University had taken my mind off those days long ago when I would sit by the wooden table in my grandma's cottage, watching her bake cakes and listening to her wild stories, so it was a complete surprise when I received a letter from her.

I need to see you.

Those words leapt off the page at me like a savage dog. I immediately thought the worst and couldn't pack my suitcase fast enough. I managed to lose myself in music for most of the journey, although every now and again my thoughts wandered to the woman who had made my childhood so magical. As I drove along the winding dirt roads, passing beneath the overhanging branches of the jacaranda and eucalypt trees, I prayed I would make it to the cottage before nightfall. I had no intention of driving through the woods after dark. It had been years since I had visited my grandma, and the woods were not a place I wanted to get lost in. I may have been twenty-one years old, but my grandma's stories of the troll under the bridge had scarred me for life.

As the sun hit the tip of the Warburton Mountains, the sky appeared to be leaking a riot of pink, orange and gold. The clouds were tinged purple, and great shadows began to creep across the fields of grass and wild daisies. I took the Reilly Road turn-off and dropped down a gear. The corrugations on the dirt track were horrendous; they always had been, although I suspected they'd become deeper over time. Then something completely unexpected happened. My car ground to a halt. Just like that, it stopped!

I looked at the fuel gauge and cursed. I'd been in such a hurry to get to Grandma Reilly's that I hadn't checked the petrol situation. I hardly used my car and had assumed it had been full from the last time I'd filled it up. Fortunately it had got me this far. It was only another mile or so to the cottage and I could call the Automobile Club when I got there.

As I walked down the road, lugging my suitcase with me, it suddenly dawned on me that I would have to cross the troll bridge; the bridge which Grandma Reilly had warned me never to use.

"Go the other way. Use the other bridge. It may take longer but at least you'll arrive in one piece."

I could hear her telling me even as I approached the rickety wooden structure, twisted and worn from decades of weather. As my eyes fell upon the familiar frame, I dropped my case and took a few minutes to scan the area for anything out of the ordinary. Cocking my head, I listened carefully, but all I could hear was the breeze through the trees and the faraway sound of water babbling over rocks. I felt rather silly but the magic in my grandma's words was powerful and a small part of me still believed in the troll.

I picked up the suitcase and put one foot forward, and then the other. Soon I had made it to the bridge, and the troll was nowhere in sight. I took a deep breath and planted a foot onto the rough wood of the bridge, half expecting something to leap out and devour me. I couldn't believe how nervous I was, and it was with great trepidation that I began to cross the bridge.

As I was moving across the middle of the bridge I caught the faintest whiff of something dead and rotting. At the same moment I heard the bridge creak, and I could have sworn I felt it lurch to one side. It may well have been my imagination playing tricks on me, but I didn't hang around to find out. I was over the bridge like lightning and I didn't even turn around to see whether or not I was being followed. Up ahead I could just make out the cottage through the tree trunks and shadows. If I could just make it to the front door, I'd be safe from both the troll and my imagination.

"Grandma Reilly?" I called out as I burst through the door.

"Is that you, Jonathon?" I heard a weak voice call from the bedroom.

"Yes, Grandma."

I walked through the warm living room, and then to the room she had slept in for more than sixty years.

"Can I come in?" I asked, poking my head around the door.

The woman I saw in my grandma's bed shocked me. Gone was the robust, rosy-cheeked woman who loved to cook, and in her place was a frail, pale stick of a person with hollow eyes and barely enough breath in her bony frame to string a sentence together.

"Well come in!" she said as I hovered by the door trying to mask my shock.

I walked to her bed and took her hand in mine.

"I got your letter," I smiled, not knowing how else to begin the conversation.

For a moment there was silence.

"I wrote you the letter because I knew you'd come," she began. "I am not long for this world and I needed to speak to you."

"Grandma!" I protested, not willing to accept the fact that she was probably right.

"Just listen," she scolded. "It's difficult to speak, but there is something I must tell you."

I sat down on the side of her bed. Her eyes were closed now and her hand sat slightly curled in mine. Her breathing became slightly deeper and her nostrils flared as if she was building up to something.

"Remember the troll under the bridge?" she asked. I said I did. "I never knew whether you believed me or not," she continued, "but I have to tell you that it is the truth. Trouble is, I never told you the entire story and I need to. I need someone to know the whole truth."

Then she stopped speaking once more to gather her thoughts and her breath. I waited without speaking, feeling that I was on the verge of learning the darkest and most important secret that had ever been.

"These woods hold many secrets. The troll under the bridge is just one of them. I've lived here for longer than I can remember, and there are places deep within its very heart that have never seen the light of day. No man has ever set foot in those parts, but on the edge of that dark heart lives a witch."

"Grandma!" I exclaimed. I had hoped she'd given up her wild stories, especially now.

A weak smile struggled onto her pale, wrinkled face, and she opened her eyes.

"My boy, a witch is nothing compared to some of the creatures that lurk in the shadows."

At that moment I heard a noise behind me, outside on the porch. I turned and thought I saw a dark shadow move by the window. I heard the loose boards of the porch floor creaking, and something knocked into the porch swing and set it rocking with such gusto that it banged rhythmically into the wall. Then the shadow passed again and I gasped as it lingered by the window, trying to peer in through the drawn curtains.

My heart began racing and my breathing deepened. What could I do against such a monster if it decided to break in? It would surely swallow us both whole. Had I locked the front door? I couldn't remember. I went to get up, adrenalin racing through my veins and giving me the courage that I needed. But as I started to stand Grandma gave my hand a slight squeeze.

"Have no fear," she said gently, moving her attention slowly towards the window and back again. "It's just your grandpa come to say goodbye."

My eyes might have been playing tricks on me, but my ears certainly weren't.

"Grandma," I began tenderly, "Grandpa is dead. In the war. Remember?"

Grandma Reilly closed her eyes and gently shook her head.

"No," she sighed. "No, he's not. That was all a terrible lie. That creature out there, pacing up and down my front porch, is your grandpa. He has come to say goodbye. He senses that I'm dying."

I was stupefied. I hardly knew what to say. Could I believe this wonderful woman who had spent her whole life weaving truth with fiction? Was this the result of a mind close to death and hallucinating?

"B-b-but how?" I stuttered. "I mean, why?"

"The witch. Jasmine Le Croux, her name was. As ugly as the day is long she was, except when she had a gentleman caller. Then she'd transform herself into a beautiful maiden using all the wicked powers she had at her disposal."

I listened, fascinated.

"As you well know, your grandpa was a tax inspector. It was part of his job to travel around the countryside collecting unpaid taxes. He was not a very popular person," she giggled. "Jasmine, due to the nature of her work, had never paid a penny of tax in her life. As you can imagine, by the time your grandpa was sent out to collect what she owed, the bill was quite considerable."

Grandma paused for breath.

"The discussion became quite heated. She refused to pay. Then your grandpa threatened to call the police on her, and that's when it happened. She used her dark powers to turn him into a troll."

"But how do you know this?" I asked. "How can you be sure?"

"Well, you see, the spell wasn't instantaneous. Not like the spells you see in cartoons. It was a gradual process. But soon after he arrived home he became too large to live inside, and then, after catching a glimpse of himself in the mirror, he decided to go and live under the bridge, away from everyone else."

With tears welling in her eyes, Grandma Reilly concluded her story.

"I know you probably don't believe me," she sobbed. "But I'd like you to do something for me. Would you let the poor soul in? He had his life with me stolen from him, so I don't want to rob him of the chance to say goodbye. I fear the time is fast approaching."

I sniffed back my own tears and tried to restrain myself from becoming too upset, but the love for my grandma, and the thought of no longer having her around, prevented me from keeping them at bay for long. I nodded and got up from the bed. As I walked to the door I watched her, lying there amongst the starched, white pillows and feather quilt, waiting for death to claim her. I could not refuse her final request no matter how difficult it was for me to open the front door and let in the grotesque creature waiting on the other side.

The troll looked me up and down, snorting as it breathed my scent in. I was like a statue. After I had stepped away from the door, I froze. Sensing I would not harm it, the troll that had haunted my nightmares all these years hesitantly entered Grandma Reilly's cottage. It plodded along slowly, sniffing the air and leaning down from its lofty height to examine the odd piece of furniture, closer to the floor. An invisible trail of stink, smelling like vomit and rot combined, followed it around like a shadow.

As it shambled into Grandma's bedroom it turned and looked at me. I stepped back again and hit the cold stone wall behind me. I smiled nervously and the creature let out a whimper before turning and disappearing around the door. I waited for a scream; instead I heard a faint giggle and then silence.

I gave them as much time as I thought they needed. I put the kettle on and made myself a cup of tea. I sat at the same wooden table I had sat at innumerable times as a child, and drank my tea. Outside it was dark. The rest of the world seemed a million miles away and suddenly I felt lonely.

It was time to go and check on Grandma.

I entered gingerly, not wanting to disturb anyone, and was shocked to find an elderly man sitting on the side of the bed, stroking grandma's hand and sobbing.

"Grandpa?" I said softly as I entered.

He looked up at me, and in his eyes I saw the truth in everything my grandma had told me. I felt a rush of shame overwhelm me.

"Yes, Jonathon. It's me."

I rushed up to him and hugged him tightly. My tears flowed freely, the happy ones with the sad. I looked over my grandpa's shoulder at the smiling face of my grandma, and knew that she had passed on. My grandpa, on the other hand, had seemingly returned from the dead.

"I've missed you," I cried. "But I wish I had you both."

Grandpa patted my back and shushed me.

"I'm afraid that could never happen," he replied. "You see, only when your grandma died could I return. The nature of the curse put on me meant we were both punished."

By now we were sobbing together and trying to offer each other words of comfort.

"At least we had a few moments together before she passed."

"What do you mean?" I asked, sitting on the bed next to him.

"There was a tiny moment after my transformation and before my darling wife passed on when I was human again. She looked into my eyes and I stared back into hers. We smiled and then she closed her eyes forever."

He looked down at his wife and spoke directly to her.

"And I wouldn't trade that moment for all the money in the world."

Originally published in Morpheus Tales #1, July 2008

Pristine By Vic Fortezza

Waiting to be called to the first tee, Adam was seated at a table in the clubhouse, eyes on the TV screen, where a senator was lauding the enactment of strict environmental safeguards.

"With these programs in place, with new technology, we've taken a huge step toward the ultimate goal of all clear-thinking citizens - a pristine environment. All man-made greenhouse gases will soon be eliminated."

Bill joined Adam, placing a streaming cup of joe atop the table. "What's goin' on?"

"Environmental perfection."

Bill waved curtly. "They can't even get the weather right. I didn't play once all winter. Global warming, my ass - it's Good Friday and it's still freezin'."

"If it wasn't for global warming, there'd be no United States of America, the greatest nation in history. Ask Siberians if it's a bad thing. These guys think the warming's gonna slow down with all these restrictions. Meanwhile, fossil fuels account for only five-percent of greenhouse gases."

"You're kiddin'," said Bill, sceptical.

"They don't want anybody to know that. It'll jeopardize what they want. Some scientists think the warming's from sunspots. Man accounts for very little of the greenhouse gases. Most come from nature, like cow farts...."

Bill tittered.

"And volcanoes and swamps."

Bill shrugged. "Fill in the swamps, black top over 'em, – and make 'em golf courses. Us baby boomers are gonna need 'em once we retire."

Adam laughed. "You'd get my vote. Trouble is, a lotta people think we're 'one' with nature. Nature could give a rat's petootie about us. That's what makes it so scary – it's completely indifferent to mankind. Earthquakes, hurricanes and lightning will kill people of all ages, creeds, colour and gender. Hopefully the environmentalists will be better at perfection than the Nazis and commies were, than the terrorists are."

"That'd be nice. At least their hearts are in the right place."

Bill's drive on the second hole bounced into the woods to the left. They found the ball immediately.

"What happened to all these trees?" said Bill, troubled. "They look dead."

Adam shrugged. "Maybe those Chinese beetles got to 'em – or were they Japanese?"

"Whatever. They shoulda used chopsticks."

Adam chuckled. "Why'm I laughin'? They might take out the whole course."

#

On Memorial Day, waiting on the 13th tee, they were buzzed by a swarm of insects. They swatted wildly with both hands.

"What the hell're they?" said Bill, looking over his clothing, brushing himself off.

"They look like somethin' you'd find in the tropics."

"Good thing we're wearin' sleeves. I'm buyin' a case of bug spray this year."

"Sometimes I think the environment's gotten so clean that species that've been dormant for decades have come back to life. A few years ago, maggots that hadn't been seen in years started chewin' up wooden piers. They must thrive in clean water."

Bill smirked. "Just what we need. I got crickets in my backyard. I haven't heard 'em since I was a kid. Sometimes I can't sleep 'cause of the racket they make. My nephew in Jersey's got bears in his backyard. He's afraid to let his kids out."

Next morning, as John was walking to the subway, he felt as if he were on a movie set, as there were so few people on the street. He had his pick of seats on the train. He assumed schools were closed.

Even the streets of Manhattan were eerily quiet. As he entered the office, he found a handful of employees huddled around a TV. There'd been an outbreak of flu. Hospitals were swamped.

"No wonder," he said.

"Thank God I got a shot," said Lois, who was 60.

Everyone present had had one. Of the firm's 25 employees, only ten made it to work.

Next day Lois called in sick. A week later she was dead, as were countless others in the nation, mostly toddlers and the aged. Doctors were baffled by the new strain, which had appeared just as the season should have been ending. By summer, millions around the world had perished. Terrorists had killed only a few thousand.

In August, waiting out the umpteenth rain delay of the season, Adam and Bill killed time watching TV in the clubhouse. Wildfires were ravaging the west. A business executive blamed environmentalists, who'd won the battle to keep certain forests untouched. The man argued that the brush, which would have been cleared by loggers, had fed the fires. Activists blamed arsonists, perhaps terrorists.

"Maybe it was the same nudniks who set fire to that development in ski country," said Bill.

"Sounds like the law of unintended consequences to me. My favourite was when they freed the minks, which wound up eating every animal in sight, and when there were none left, turned on each other."

Bill laughed and looked to the TV.

"Another thing is the bio-diesel craze. There's so much money to be made that forests are bein' cleared to grow the stuff that's turned into the fuels. It's the exact opposite of what the zealots want, unintended consequences again. When DDT was banned it was supposed to save people from cancer. Meanwhile, millions of Africans have died from malaria since then. No way even a tiny fraction of that would've died from the big C. And they still won't let Africans use the stuff. It's crazy."

Bill had stopped listening. Adam stifled himself.

"On a more positive note," said the anchorman, "officials report that the ozone layer, thought to have been damaged beyond repair, is closing at a rapid rate. Cases of skin cancer are expected to plummet. Activists cite this as one of the benefits of the elimination of greenhouse gases."

Adam and Bill let out a subdued mock cheer.

By next season tee time reservation was no longer necessary, as people were avoiding wooded areas. Adam occasionally had the entire course to himself. Bill no longer played, citing his wife and kids. Adam missed his friend's cheerfulness and sense of humour. For the first time in his adult life he did not regret not having a family. He imagined how worried parents must be, despite the assurances of doctors and politicians, as disease was increasing at an alarming rate.

The beach season was brief, as the area's waters attracted mysterious predators, which, soon lacking bathers to devour, resorted to feeding on their neighbours, which ruined the fishing. And insects moved from the woods to the streets, which drove people indoors behind closed windows and sealed doors. Many who did not have air-conditioning suffered heatstroke and were hospitalized. Some went mad, leaping from fire escapes and rooftops.

For a while theatres were packed. Soon rats invaded, causing panic in some venues. Those who remained activists insisted that other species had as much right to the planet as humans. One, interviewed on a street corner, was chased into traffic by a mob and struck by a truck. Police had to beat back the dogs that feasted on her remains. The incident was captured on film. Another activist said it proved which was the most dangerous species.

Bear, deer and wolves were spotted in Central Park, in Forest Park in Queens and Prospect Park in Brooklyn. Games at Yankee and Shea Stadium were interrupted, as trained handlers had to be summoned to corral the beasts. The sparse crowds booed lustily. All businesses suffered except those that manufactured bug spray or guns. From March to November people sprayed themselves from head to foot. Incidences of skin cancer rose dramatically.

Backlash began with human predators, criminals, who made sport of shooting animals. An occasional stray bullet found a bystander. The ugly element thrived as civic resources were depleted, at first by recession, then depression, despite the enormous savings on social security and Medicare realized because of the death of so many of the elderly. The police force was stretched thin.

Those in dire straits fed their families venison. Those who hadn't abandoned the city went hunting at night, using homemade spears. Some were mauled by animals. The stench of rotting flesh was prevalent throughout the world's large cities. Activists, diminishing in number each day, decried the savagery of man.

When dead rats began turning up everywhere, politicians found their spines. Tens of millions were dying around the globe. The price of food skyrocketed as corn was being used to make ethanol. This led to riots in developing countries. The hardcore activists lamented that environmental restrictions hadn't been implemented soon enough, that the eco-disaster they'd long predicted had finally arrived. Soon they disappeared or went underground. One pundit quipped that they'd joined the list of endangered species.

When the forests were made barren, the beetles turned to telephone poles, confounding scientists. Utility companies, understaffed, were unable to keep up with demand. Cities were frequently plunged into darkness for days. Looting was commonplace - until there was nothing left to loot. Those politicians unable to afford bodyguards armed themselves. Some were killed, others killed in self-defence. Government buildings were vandalized, eventually abandoned.

#

Adam, now 65, long out of work, had not left his building in years, since depleting his savings. He'd travelled as far as the lobby to retrieve his mail. When it'd stopped coming, he no longer left his floor. He lived on the rats he caught and cooked. At times he went days without nourishment. Fortunately the water was as clean as it'd ever been.

He no longer feared eviction. He wondered if the landlord had died or simply abandoned the property. He didn't hear much movement and suspected he was the last tenant in the building, which had housed hundreds.

The sun shined brightly beyond his windows. If not for the media, he would not have known of the horror outside.

His phone went first. Even his cell phone stopped working. He was no longer able to log on to the internet. He lost contact with relatives and friends. When his TV died, he relied exclusively on the radio, as newspaper delivery had ceased. He clung to life even when gas was no longer delivered to the stove. He cooked rats over fires he built in other apartments. He was constantly searching for matches, which in winter saved him, as there was no other means to provide heat, or to warm water for bathing or washing clothes. He shaved his head to maintain cleanliness.

One day there was only static on the radio, then dead air. Eventually nothing came out of the tap.

Sand wedge in hand, he chose to go outside to die. It was not a tough decision, as he hadn't much of a life and he'd relinquished hope that things would get better.

There was a pond several inches deep in the lobby. The water main had burst, buckling and cracking open the asphalt. The only living things Adam saw were rats, dogs and cats. The street looked as if a bomb had landed on it. There was not a trace of smog in the air, however. The environment was pristine save for the stench of death, which he supposed would dissipate once man was extinct.

He chuckled as he came upon his car. It'd been brutalized by vandals - and there were parking tickets, weathered by the elements, stacked under a windshield wiper. Priorities, he thought, shaking his head.

He was followed by dogs - or were they wolves? His vision had deteriorated during his seclusion. His hearing was fine, as the cackling above him was loud and clear. There were vultures in the sky - in Brooklyn. Will wonders ever cease, he said to himself ironically.

He felt the sting of mosquitoes and knew it would not be long. Although he was too weak to protect himself, he held on to the sand wedge, hoping it would deter the animals, have them wait until he was dead before they began gnawing on him. He would have liked to die on the golf course, but it was too far. Besides, he was certain it would be unrecognizable, wild with growth.

He sat at the curb and stared back at the animals that were sizing him up. He imagined they were drooling. "Dinner's on," he thought, the phrase his mother had used to summon him from the street. He was glad she hadn't lived to see this.

As the animals inched closer, he chuckled, and wished for once he were an environmental activist.

They'd probably spit you out, he thought.

Originally published in Morpheus Tales #1, July 2008

He Said Something By Todd Austin Hunt

When I met Satan, I was inside Sav-a-Bunch on the corner of Rimwall and Wellington, waiting in the slowest fucking line ever to pay for my gas, water and chocolate pie. My head was fucking killing me. I was thirsty as hell, and even though it was only closing in on nine am, my mouth tasted like some dying dog took a shit in it. Me and Josh Gunther finished off a fifth of Beam the night before.

Oh, yeah. My name's Josh Gunther.

Well, I killed most of it, but about an inch soaked my fucking crotch when I fell asleep with the bottle in my hand. That morning I was almost not drunk. It wouldn't matter whether I was drunk, sober or dead. My job was a damn joke. I was a security guard at the Russet County Public Library. I'm taller than most guys, and my arms are bigger than most guys' necks. All I have to do is walk around the damn place, look mean, and sometimes touch my gun when some asshole acts up. Mostly it's the fucking kids. I hate those fucking kids. One time, I caught this little skinny kid with his wanker out, pissing on the carpet in a dark corner of the non-fiction racks. You should have seen his face. He was scared like all get out. I made him get down on his knees and stick his nose in it, like some dumbass puppy. I knew he wouldn't tell; he was too scared.

Anyways, there were three morons in front of me, and in exactly one minute I was late for work. I cussed under my breath, but the woman directly in front of me heard. Her fat head swung around. The folds of fat hanging from her face and neck followed a couple seconds later. She frowned at me, and her wet mouth opened.

"God hears every word," she said to me.

That pissed me off. "Turn around, and stuff a couple handfuls of those Cheetos in your mouth, ma'am. That'll surely stop it up." I grinned and nodded at her, as if I was giving her helpful advice. Her jaw snapped shut, and her chin disappeared in a fat and a freakish overbite. She turned away, and I heard a squeaky whimper.

Stupid, fat bitch.

A college kid with greasy hair was in front of her. He was staring at me, starting to get angry. I touched my piece and the anger changed to something else. He looked at the floor in front of him, tapping his hardpack Camels against his waist.

I was too thirsty. I couldn't wait anymore. I ripped the top off my water and guzzled the whole fucking bottle. My headache got even worse from the cold. It didn't do me any damn good, though. I was still thirsty, like there was some kind of forest fire in my stomach.

The line hadn't moved a bit. A girl with an ass the size of a beach ball leaned up against the counter, chattering like a squirrel with the cashier. She didn't even have anything to buy, and the bitch was wasting my fucking time talking to some buck-toothed loser with a crew-cut and a huge zit on his right ear. I couldn't understand what they were talking about, just a bunch of goddamn noise that was pounding into my headache like a nightstick into Rodney King.

"Come on," I said. "Hurry the fuck up!"

All of them looked at me like I was some genital wart. But only for a moment. The girl and the cashier continued talking, ignoring me. The empty plastic bottle crumpled in my hands, and my chocolate pie burst open, its guts dripped out, and plopped down onto my boots. I just shined those boots the day before.

I was gonna say something else, but the door opened. A bell chimed, but the cashier and everybody else didn't even look to see who it was. I did. It was the weirdest looking guy I've ever seen. From the neck down, he was huge. He wore a jogging suit, and it looked like the fabric was in serious pain trying to hold back his fucking muscles, which rippled and moved constantly underneath. That made me think of a rattlesnake when it moves across the ground. But his neck and head were the creepy part. His neck was shrivelled, a dark thing that looked like a root. His face was narrow, cheeks hollow, as if he hadn't had anything to eat for days. His eyes were a dark green, and huge bags sagged beneath them. He was bald, and gross looking liver-spots covered his scalp. He didn't have any lips.

He opened his mouth, and smiled at me. His teeth were painfully white. Painful. It hurt my eyes; I had to squint. When he smiled at me, I dropped the smashed pie and the bottle. God, I've never felt so fucking good in my life. It was like the blood running through my veins had turned to one hundred percent pure smack.

And then he said something. It was real quick and short, and I couldn't hear it because the dumbass girl wouldn't shut her fucking mouth. I had to hear what the man said. Had to. If I didn't, I felt like I'd go crazy.

"What did you say?" I pleaded. "Please, repeat what you just said!"

His mouth was closed. He wasn't smiling at me anymore. My skin started to itch, and my joints began to hurt like hell. His eyes darted over to the girl. I followed his gaze. She flipped back her bleach-blond hair with her hand, never ceasing the yapping. I glared at the line of her jaw as it moved. She was just a fucking cow without the cud in her mouth.

"Shut up," I said quietly. Then I screamed. "*Shut the fuck up!*"

I only saw her surprised expression for a moment, because a bullet from my nine-millimetre sheared off most of the top of her head, and whatever she was thinking of saying next sprayed all over the cashier's face. A chunk of brain oozed to the tip of his nose and splattered onto the counter.

It was quiet for a second, and I turned to the man again, waiting for him to speak. Once he opened his mouth though, the cashier, the fat preacher lady and the college kid, erupted in shrieks. The lady began to choke on something. I think it was vomit. That shut her up a bit. She collapsed on the floor, her face turning purple. She moved around a little bit. Not that long, really.

The cashier's mouth had become a huge hole in his stupid face. His hand was below the counter, pushing something. The screams were an ice pick in my brain. Both those guys screamed like little girls; they reminded me of those fucking kids at the library. The college kid yanked at his dirty hair. Without taking his eyes from me, he leaped toward the door. He didn't even see the man who was trying to say something. The kid passed right through him, and pushed himself out of the store.

The man at the door shuddered as the kid went through him. His eyes closed for a moment, and a wet, black thing slipped from his mouth and licked his phantom lips. The kid outside froze on the sidewalk. He walked a bit to the right of the door, and stepped up to the glass, pressing his face against it, staring inside with a blank look on his face. He beat his head repeatedly against the surface. When he finally dropped, he left a gross smear.

The cashier wouldn't quit screaming. I approached the counter, and he backed up against the wall. His screams took the form of words. "Don't kill me! Don't kill me!"

I wanted to get right up to the counter, but the dead bitch he was talking to was in the way. Cursing, I bent down and grabbed the corpse by the front of her Levis, and hurled her out of the way. I leaned on the counter. "Quit screaming," I said calmly, pissed off as fuck. With my free hand, I pointed to the man at the door. "Can't you see the man is trying to say something? He's got something important to say to me, and because you won't be quiet, he won't talk."

The cashier looked at the door, but, like the college kid, he didn't see anything. Whatever little patience I had was fucking used up.

"Shit," I said. I jumped onto the counter on my knees and grabbed the little dumbass by his shirt, yanking him close. His shrieks got louder and higher. I stuffed the barrel of my gun into his giant mouth, which muffled his noise a little bit. Tears rolled down his face, getting my hand wet.

"Damn."

I switched hands for a moment so I could wipe my hand on my shirt. Since the little bastard didn't have any hair, I had to grab him by his ear. I felt that massive pimple burst against my fingers, which pissed me off even more. "Don't scream anymore," I said quietly. "I want to hear this man speak. Shut up."

No. He didn't stop.

"Shit." Letting go of his ear, I pushed the gun deep into his mouth and pulled the trigger. His head exploded. The cigarettes above and behind him caught most of the dumb shit's blood and thoughts. I didn't get any on me. I holstered my gun. Taking my handkerchief from my pocket, I wiped the pus and blood off my fingers, and tossed it on the cashier's body.

It was finally quiet. I got down from the counter, my boots smacking against the floor. I walked over to the man at the door. He hadn't moved a bit. The man was tall. I had to fucking look up to see his eyes. In the distance, I heard sirens approaching. People were starting to crowd around outside. It wasn't going to be quiet for long.

    I looked up at the man and smiled. He grinned down at me.

    "Finally," I said. "I thought those fuckheads would never be quiet."

    He was silent.

    "Well, what was it you said to me? I have to know what you said."

    His lipless mouth cracked open. His voice sounded like a rake on asphalt. "I didn't say anything."

    I felt my chin fall.

    "What?" I said. "You're a liar. You're a fucking *liar*."

Originally published in Morpheus Tales #1, July 2008

The Sliding By Kevin Lucia

November, 2007

I've broken a promise made long ago, and I don't know what's going to happen.

The cursor on my IMAC blinks, daring me to continue what I'd started months ago. What once seemed safe, now felt foolish. I was dancing at the edge of something terrible, but I didn't know if I could stop, or wanted to, for that matter.

Maybe it's the long nights, which have only become more desolate since Jennifer packed her bags and left, or the cold bed I wake up in every morning. Maybe it's driving to work and eating alone; or maybe it's the dead eyes looking back at me from the mirror, dull and flat.

I called Joel and Chris the other day, but the conversation fizzled. They remember three high school kids trespassing in an old house, nothing more. Even with gentle prodding, I couldn't get their shuttered memories past a certain point. To them, nothing happened.

However, something did happen. One August Saturday afternoon we glimpsed a dark, powerful truth: that a shadowed world exists next to ours, one that defies explanation.

Slowly, my fingers engaged the keys, initially hesitant, but with each keystroke the corridors in my mind widened. With care, I again opened doors shut long ago, wondering if tonight the things sliding in the dark would claim me at last.

#

August, 1985

I hesitated on the old porch outside the closed window, hand resting lightly on cracked siding. Through dirty glass the room appeared empty, littered with the debris you'd expect in an abandoned house.

"This's stupid," I breathed. "You seriously want to do this?"

I couldn't see, but heard the smirk in Joel's voice. "C'mon, you're the biggest guy here. Don't tell me you're chicken."

I glared at him over my shoulder. Joel and I'd been friends since kindergarten, but sometimes he pissed me off. I'm cautious by nature and he's not, especially when I'm going first.

"Listen, you may not have football this fall, but I do. I don't want to miss the season because I sliced myself on a broken window messing around."

"Honestly, Joel," Chris said, leaning against the siding, "that window wasn't closed up last summer. Maybe this isn't smart."

Chris's support emboldened me. "Okay, we can open this - I'm just gonna need a hand, because the frame's weak, and I don't want the glass to break." I grasped one corner of the window, and nodded at the other. "Chris...?"

He nodded, moving quickly, without second thought.

As we carefully tried to open the window, I asked, "So what's the deal with this place?"

The story was typical. Bassler House was an old, three storey Victorian that had stood abandoned for years, and every summer when Chris and his brother visited their grandmother at Clifton Lake, they took a pilgrimage here to test their mettle. According to Chris, its walls and floors were adorned with hastily scrawled Satan-worshiping paraphernalia: pentagrams, 666 and predictable slogans such as 'Satan Rulz' and 'Jesus Suks'.

"It's lame," Chris finished as the window opened, "it was fun to poke around as kids, but there's not much here."

"That's only because we haven't gone into the basement yet," Joel remarked from behind.

I glanced at the crumbling foundation and remarked, "That's probably smart."

Joel snorted at what he probably thought was cowardice; but I ignored him, knowing the only way he'd venture into the basement would be if I went first.

Thank God we didn't go into the basement that day; because I don't believe we would've made it out of there.

Seconds later, after crawling through the window, I stood in the middle of a musty smelling room on the first floor. Wallpaper peeled from the walls in shrivelled strips like used-up snake-skin, the floor covered with gritty dust, corners piled with crushed soda cans, broken beer bottles, a headless doll here, a broken plate there.

An open door stood in the corner.

"So the stuff's in the other room?"

"Yeah," Joel drawled, "check it out... if you got the guts."

Chris sighed as he climbed in after me. "You're an ass."

Joel's reply was brilliant in its eloquence. "Bite me."

I ignored them, approaching the far room. A feeling lingered in the air, exerting a slight pressure I felt in my ears and head. Maybe all abandoned houses were like this, haunted by the memories of their former occupants.

Bassler House held more than memories.

I stepped through the door and stopped, arrested by what I saw.

In the room beyond was the much-rumoured pentagram - but it wasn't hastily scrawled on the wall, nor did it appear the work of drunken college students. Planted with the meticulous care of only the most committed was a brick-laid pentagram, roughly the size of the room.

It was a near-perfect circle.

At that point, Chris reached my shoulder. "Holy... "

Still on the porch, Joel swiped a broken tree branch, wedged it between windowsill and window, and scrambled through. "What's up?" He joined Chris at my back, stopped, and muttered, "Damn."

I glanced at him. "That's never been there before?"

Chris, breathless. "No freakin' way."

Joel, numb. "Uh-uh."

Of course, we did the next, most logical thing: we walked slowly around it.

Instantly, a putrid smell hit my nostrils, a high-pitched buzz I hadn't noticed before in the air. Squinting, I saw above each pentagram triangle a mass of flies, and as I passed them, a rotten smell wafted upwards, making me taste bile.

Several somethings had apparently been sacrificed here - or at the very least, someone wanted people to think so.

I never saw what rotted in those triangles, and to this day, I'm glad. I tell myself 'squirrel' or 'mouse', and I'm content.

We made our circuit and found ourselves clustered by a winding stairway leading to the second and third floors. The whiteness of my friend's faces told me enough: the pentagram was something they'd never seen before.

Stating the obvious, Chris whispered, "This is new."

I believed Chris's sincerity, but prodded Joel, who was prone to arranging elaborate pranks, "You didn't do this?"

The shock on his face was unnerving. Though Joel often talked with exaggerated flair, he was no coward. "No way," he muttered, the corners of his mouth drawn tight.

Someone had painted the room's walls white, and the blankness felt alien, out of place. No debris collected here, and with the exception of the pentagram, the flies and stench, the room was practically sterile.

However, as no black-robed Satanists slid from hidden crevices to offer us as virgin sacrifices, (which we'd be, despite our grandiose lies to each other), we relaxed. We figured the pentagram was the creation of some lonely Goth kids with nothing better to do; the buzzing flies feasting on rotten hamburger, not animals. We couldn't explain the whiteness of the room, so we dismissed it.

Of course, the best thing to do in a situation like this is something stupid; because that always helps chase away cold sweats. After sharing very mundane explanations, Joel flashed his trademark grin. "We should wreck it."

I glanced at Chris. "You mean... "

"Sure. Toss the bricks out the window; screw up their little Goth-Satanist party." He raised his eyebrows pointedly. "God would want us to, dontcha think?"

If you've never been raised country-Baptist, such a challenge means nothing. However, both Joel and I had deacons for fathers, and though an Episcopalian, Chris had attended Afton Baptist with us for three years. The idea of God using us to smite the forces of lonely, Goth-Satan worshipers was absurd, yet oddly empowering.

This time I wasn't content to lead. "Fine," I nodded at the bricks, "be my guest."

Joel's eyes narrowed. For a moment, I thought he'd pass.

In a flash he grinned, vaulted to the pentagram, grabbed a brick, and flung it with rare enthusiasm at the room's only window.

The brick crashed through the glass with a righteous sound.

The next few minutes are hazy in my memory. When hordes of Satanists didn't stream forth to devour us, we descended upon the pentagram, driven, grabbing and chucking bricks through the window in a whirlwind of arms and legs.

I don't remember much except our flashing, twisted faces, howling mouths, burning eyes. We tossed, grabbed, threw - moving like manic machines.

I hate to think that in our fervour we scooped up the rotten masses in the pentagram's triangles with our bare hands, but we must've, because when the moment passed, the floor lay bare - though smeared in places.

Minutes later, we stood in the room's centre, panting, shirts soaked with sweat - though it wasn't hot. As our adrenaline ebbed, we eyed each other with dreadful fascination. We'd lost ourselves in the brick-throwing frenzy, the fervour of which was alarming.

We stood there in the tired weirdness, waiting.

Joel broke the silence by clapping his hands with authority, saying, "Well, that's that. Let's go see if there's anything cool upstairs."

Suddenly, Bassler House was nothing more than an old house in need of exploring. Our momentary fugue dismissed, we tramped up the winding stairs in search of more oddities.

Ten to fifteen minutes later, we descended, deflated. We hadn't found much; most of the rooms were empty save scraps of litter, offering little amusement. Perhaps the most interesting things we'd found was a dented, pitted whisky flask in one third floor room, and in a second floor room, the entire floor had caved in, causing us to speculate if man or animal had plunged to their deaths through the gaping hole.

I'm not sure how we didn't see it as we came down, but the smell hit us the instant our feet found the bottom step.

"What the hell... " Joel breathed.

There, in the middle of the room, was the pentagram, untouched, as if we'd never destroyed it. The flies buzzed as before, and when our collective eyes travelled to the window we'd thrown the bricks through...

"The window," I croaked, "it's not broken."

From our position, we saw the window we'd crawled through, and Chris pointed a shaking finger, managing, "The window we came in is closed."

"We left it open. Joel propped it open!"

I can tell you nothing of what happened next. Though we clambered towards our exit, seconds later we found ourselves standing around the pentagram, each at a triangle tip facing the other, rotten somethings buzzing at our feet with hordes of flies.

We couldn't move or speak; we stood clenched in fear. I'll never forget the sweaty sheen on Joel's forehead; the tendons straining in Chris's neck, and my fingernails digging into my palms.

Nor will I forget the slithering, shuffling, sliding, coming from the far hallway, and, though it lasted forever, it never got any closer.

Finally, Joel grated, "Wreck it. Gotta...wreck it."

They were magic words, breaking the spell. We again descended upon the pentagram. I remember our strange, twisted faces, howling mouths, burning eyes. We grabbed and threw bricks through the window again.

When we finished, Joel clapped his hands and said, "Well, that's that. Let's go see if there's anything cool upstairs."

Again we ascended, descended, and when we hit bottom the stench of decayed meat assailed our nostrils as Joel breathed...

"What the hell?"

"The window's not broken."

"Where we came in - it's closed. Joel propped it open, I know he did!"

We tried to run, but found ourselves rooted again around the pentagram, as something slowly slid down the hallway - much closer this time.

We fought, struggled, sweat, ground our teeth until finally Joel managed, "Wreck it. Gotta... wreck it."

Once again we did, only to find ourselves returned to our spots, the slithering and shuffling and sliding closer.

After the same interminable fight, Joel choked, "Wreck it. Gotta... wreck it."

I found my voice. "No! Leave it!"

Joel and Chris looked at me, eyes wide, disbelieving. "We have to," Joel hissed, "it's making this happen!"

Something seized me, an increasing pressure banging inside my head. My ears rang and eyes watered, and I wanted to destroy the pentagram so bad my hands itched with desire.

The house didn't want me to talk. I don't know how I knew that, or how it was possible, but it was true all the same.

I managed to shake my head. "No…it wants us to keep wrecking it…to stay stuck. It's holding us here…for something."

Shocked realization lit in their eyes. Chris nodded, wincing. "The sound in the hallway… it's getting closer."

My mind whirled, and I felt sick; my head pounded and I tasted more bile, but I pressed on, following my intuition.

"We leave it," I gasped, fighting tears. "Go away, and don't tell anyone."

"We'll forget."

The pressure disappeared, our bodies free.

The sounds in the hallway, however... were closer.

"Go!"

We pounded away from the pentagram, arms and legs pistoning, and into the adjoining room. With the loop broken, the window was propped open as Joel had left it, but as we fled the slithering, sliding sound filled the room, and I'm sure each of us - as I did - felt the hot mist of some dark creature's breath on our necks

Joel, faster than Chris and I, scrambled through the window first, knocked away the untrustworthy branch holding up the rickety window, and braced it open with his arm.

I've always wondered if he glimpsed what pursued us, because I remember his white face and dinner-plate eyes as he screamed, "It's coming!"

Chris made it through the window easily. I slid to a stop, my tall, lanky frame prone to clumsiness, and I easily saw myself bringing the window down upon me, shattered glass and all.

I put my hands and one foot on the windowsill to pull myself through...

... and stopped.

I wanted to turn around, and see it for what it was.

Something in me needed to.

Doing as they would for years to come - saving me from myself - Chris and Joel grabbed my shoulders and pulled me through the window. We crashed together on the old, weakened porch in a dusty heap, rotten boards groaning but not breaking. The window shut with a resounding bang, somehow not shattering.

The air fell still.

It was over.

We glanced at each other for several quiet minutes.

... won't tell a-anyone...

... we'll forget...

"We should get going," Chris offered, "Dad'll have the grill hot by now."

"Yeah," Joel added, "and Bonnie wanted to go into town before dinner."

I nodded, saying nothing. We got up, brushed the dust off our clothes, and walked away from Bassler House, ignoring the much lower sun; ignoring also the muted sound of something shuffling, slithering, sliding in the dark.

November, 2007

I sat back in my chair, flexing my fingers. My agent had bugged me for months about starting a novel, saying it's time to graduate from short stories. He says I've got Bram Stoker Award, and Stephen King, Joe Hill, and Peter Straub written all over me.

This will never be published. I'd started it for myself, for understanding, closure, maybe meaning. It would make a great novel, but I'd already partly reneged on my promise, and didn't dare revoke it entirely.

... we'll forget...

When I don't write, I sleep well, but when I can't hold it inside any longer and hold an evening confessional with my IMAC, all through that night something shuffles and slides its way down the hallway towards my bedroom; shuffling, slithering, sliding, but never getting any closer. I imagine it'll stay that way, so long as I keep the rest of the promise.

We won't tell anyone.

I shut down the IMAC, and headed off to sleep - hoping to God I hadn't gone too far already, and the sliding wouldn't come any closer tonight.

Originally published in Morpheus Tales #1, July 2008

The Darkest Of Waters By Tommy B. Smith

Tsiatis stood on the deck and gazed out across the ocean, and the cold brine sprayed lightly onto him, a vivid reminder that it was far too late to turn back now. The crew had laboured for months to traverse the majesty of the ocean, and as the ship neared its destination, the ominous hour of resolution loomed within reach.

His hands came to rest on the rail, and his luminescent eyes turned toward his associates across the deck. He tolerated their company for now, as a necessity, but he could not bring himself to trust either of them. Hessan was a human, and Dytus was a colocom. Though Tsiatis had little experience with those of either race, he knew well their harsh roles in the history of Megola.

Tsiatis was kanalora; his light features, and especially the glimmer of his eyes, were evidence to this, even from a considerable distance. He carried himself with dignity and refined grace, which was more than he could expect of his colleagues, most notably the colocom.

The incandescent eyes of Tsiatis were drawn to a spot on the water's surface. The water had rippled, and there had been movement.

There was a splash, and something lurched upward into plain view. Tsiatis almost jumped. He saw then that it was only a shark, incapable of damaging the massive ship, and harmless to all aboard from its position so far below. Nonetheless, it had surprised him, and it only affirmed his tension. He glanced at Dytus, and saw the colocom's reptilian eyes looking back at him. He expected some derisive comment, but the colocom looked back to the ocean without a word.

Tsiatis never held any of the colocom in high regard. They were known to be a savage, destructive race. The kanalora had never been disposed to such base motivations. In war lay the future ruin of the world, as had nearly been the case numerous times throughout history.

Still, the current goals of Tsiatis and Dytus were the same. They had united for the same purpose, and their stakes in the voyage were equal. Both of them, and Hessan as well, had taken on the phenomenal financial burden. They had formed the binding commitment to sail directly into the heart of the world, where the oldest secrets of Megola stemmed at the dawn of time, to Megola's lost, and most ancient, continent of Norbain.

"Dark skies ahead," called the lookout from above. "Unsafe waters within view." Hessan nodded, then turned to look at Dytus and Tsiatis.

"It's the Barrier," he said grimly. "It's still a fair distance, but it's in sight." The captain pushed his damp hair away from his face. Tsiatis nodded brusquely, and the colocom barely acknowledged the captain's statement. All three of them knew the risk ahead, as the ship sailed timidly onward, and the fury of the skies and sea crashed with volatile rage in the distance.

Tsiatis was aware of what had befallen past attempts to bypass the Barrier; he owned a small book filled with such accounts. It documented ocean voyages like this one, wherein a worthy crew was assembled to travel the span of the oceans, to penetrate the ever-present Barrier, and reach the secluded continent of Norbain. The book held third-person accounts, compiled by parties affiliated with the voyages in various ways. The captains, and crews themselves, had been swallowed up in the Barrier, and all logs they kept had disappeared with them.

What distinguished this voyage from the others was the inclusion of two magi of exceptional prowess. Tsiatis had studied magic most of his life, and had a tremendous respect for the Gift. The colocom, Dytus, was also versed in magic, but the colocom's expertise was mainly associated with battle magic. Tsiatis had always appreciated magic as an art form and a preserved form of culture. He held distaste for those who considered it as nothing more than a weapon.

Tsiatis and Dytus hoped to counteract the perils of the Barrier with the combined use of their magic, at least long enough for the ship to pass through the deadly field. Though he was a human, and unfamiliar with magic as well, Hessan was a very reputable captain. His ship was touted as one of the best constructed. After lengthy discussions over this incredible task, their grudging partnership began, though their motivations were widely separate.

Tsiatis distrusted the colocom's motives the most. Tsiatis certainly did not want the powers of the old land to be wasted in the endless war between the colocom and the xevax, but he knew that most colocom were fiercely loyal to their own. Dytus was likely no exception. Dytus never spoke much, and Tsiatis could only speculate on what thoughts might be littering his reptilian head.

The kanalora mage knew that, if the three reached the shores of Norbain, the truths would come out. Until then, there was no point in dissecting the possibilities. First, they would have to survive the Barrier.

"The dark waters are almost upon us," Hessan spoke. He turned and walked briskly to the helm to relieve the first mate. To the mild surprise of Tsiatis, Dytus retired to his private quarters.

The ship glided across the calm waters toward the impending devastation of the Barrier's waters. During the wait, Tsiatis relaxed himself as best he could manage, and worked to clear his mind in preparation. Hessan stood at the ship's helm and stared across the waters toward what awaited. At the last moment, Dytus emerged from his quarters and returned to the deck.

The ship sailed into the churning waters beneath the blackened sky, and passed into the Barrier of Norbain.

Hessan was as adept a captain and helmsman as one could imagine, but he was hard-pressed to keep the ship steady in such turbulent waters. He fought the winds' defiance and the explosive anger of the waters to pull the ship through. The crew scrambled across the deck like mad ants in their frenzy to obey their captain's barking orders, to save this voyage, and to secure their own lives.

Tsiatis stood near the colocom, at the deck rail. Dytus glanced at him, but still remained unemotional, and appeared impartial to the rapid development of the situation.

Though Hessan was not the most hygienic fellow, Tsiatis could not dispute the human's mastery while at sea. Hessan's skilled crew was highly organized under his command, and the captain expertly guided the ship through the waters of the Barrier with precision. Still, as Tsiatis looked on from his position, the kanalora could not expel the doubt and fear from his mind.

The storm worsened within a matter of seconds. The tides were powerful and persistent. Hessan fought with all his might to turn the ship's rudder against the ocean's opposition. The substantial ferocity of the winds continued to increase. The ship swayed and tumbled, and seawater cascaded all around.

Both Tsiatis and Dytus gripped the rail with harsh firmness to avoid being thrown across the deck. There was a cry of desperation as one of the crew was flung overboard. Hessan cursed loudly as he struggled to right the ship against the madness of the storm.

The thunder that bombarded everyone's ears was deafening. Lightning streaked through the black abyss of the sky. The awful din grew, and the sky crackled with deadly energies. Even Hessan was cowed by the fury in the sky, and of the elements that now conspired. The ship, and all aboard it, seemed diminutive and fragile in comparison to the twisted wrath of the Barrier.

With a start, Tsiatis could now see shapes beneath the waves. The darkness of the water was not enough to obscure the horrific outlines just beneath its surface, shapes which did not correlate with any conceivable archetype of natural ocean life. Tsiatis looked over at Dytus, and saw that his yellow, serpentine eyes were scanning the ocean as well. From the colocom's tightly clenched jaw, it was apparent that he also saw the menacing abnormalities beginning to rise from the water.

The motion of the unidentified anomalies halted at the water's surface, and they appeared to be spreading out in vast numbers. They surrounded the ship and closed in from every angle. What were they? Were they merely sea life, conjoined in focus by the overwhelming forces of the barrier, or were they something terrible and different, which Tsiatis had never before witnessed? Tsiatis's dread grew, and he knew that he had to act.

Tsiatis launched into the casting of a spell. Dytus had already done the same. The golden magical energy rained down into the waters as each of them bombarded the creatures beneath the waves with destructive magic.

After both the kanalora and the colocom had released their assault on the ocean's unknown denizens, the waters began to boil angrily, and it became apparent that the magical attack had done little or no harm. Worse, it seemed to have agitated them, and they closed in on the ship with crazed fervour.

There was a shattering explosion from within the midst of the ship's crew. One of the ship's sails went ablaze, struck by lightning. Dytus moved into another spell, and released an icy torrent of frost upon the sail to extinguish the flames.

Tsiatis was trying to formulate another plan of attack on the creatures of the ocean, but his thoughts were interrupted by a loud roaring sound from beneath the deck. Hessan turned from the ship's helm in horror, and the kanalora looked to him in confusion.

"The ship's going down!" he bellowed. Tsiatis felt a sickening lurch in his stomach. The hull of the ship had been penetrated, and the roaring noise had been the sound of the ocean's water rushing into the ship's hold.

The things in the water had broken through the thick hull. The ship was filling with water. Hessan, the captain who had fared bravely in many terrible storms, was powerless. The ship was going to sink, and all of them would die.

Tsiatis fought to suppress the panic mounting within him. He looked toward the colocom. Dytus stood firm and continued to don his mask of steel, but he was afraid, Tsiatis knew, just as the rest of them were.

The ship began to break apart as it was devoured by the ocean. The ship capsized and was torn into worthless segments. Tsiatis was flung through the air. Hessan was set upon by legions of the unknown creatures, and Tsiatis was not able to see what befell the doomed captain then. Perhaps it was fitting, Tsiatis thought, as he plunged into the freezing waters.

Tsiatis tried to fight the tides and swim to the surface. If he could reach the surface, he could intone a spell to protect himself, and hopefully save himself from the deadly creatures of the ocean. Even if he succeeded, how long could he last in the waters of the Barrier? How long could he maintain the spell, and how long could he swim before the ocean drank his soul to the bottom of its depths, as it had innumerable others throughout history?

Tsiatis somehow reached the surface and began to gasp for air. He knew it would only be a matter of seconds before he was pulled under again; he simply did not have the strength to last. The Barrier would claim yet another victim, and he would go quietly along with Hessan, Dytus, and the rest of the ship's crew.

A cold hand closed over the kanalora's wrist. The hand felt coarse against his skin, and its grip was strong. He saw another hand reach for him, and he saw that it was gray and reptilian in appearance. He reached out for his colocom rescuer. With a firm tug, Dytus pulled Tsiatis from the water.

"You are alive," Tsiatis breathed, still labouring to fill his lungs with fresh oxygen. He and Dytus sat on a large piece of the drifting wood from the ship. It teetered back and forth with the addition of the new weight, but remained afloat.

The colocom had never been such a welcome sight to Tsiatis. He realized now that he had sorely misjudged the colocom. Regardless of differences, Dytus was a loyal comrade, and Tsiatis began to regret his initial judgment of the colocom.

The perilous waters of the Barrier did not discriminate. Tsiatis and Dytus were both at the Barrier's mercy now, clinging to a remnant of the destroyed ship, and a last trace of hope.

"There is no time," Dytus stated with urgency. "We must combine our defensive magics, so that they cannot get to us."

By they, Tsiatis knew that Dytus meant the things which had rent the ship apart. The kanalora and the colocom were more vulnerable than ever as they clung to the piece of floating rubbish. It would surely not be long before the ocean finished with the remains of the ship and crew, and moved on to the two of them.

Tsiatis and Dytus clasped hands for the casting of the spell, to magnify its strength and reduce its toll on each of them. A field of protective magic surrounded their wooden means of floatation.

"I do not know how long we can last out here," Tsiatis said, looking at the sky and at the waters, while the broken wood that supported both of them was tossed around at the casual mercy of nature's warped amusement.

The colocom said nothing for a moment, and then his stoic facade finally crumbled. "Nor do I, kanalora," he admitted.

Dytus was visibly exhausted from the petrifying ordeal they had experienced. Tsiatis knew he would be unable to cast another spell without allowing his focus on the magical protective field to lapse. He had his doubts that he could even maintain it much longer without giving way to fatigue.

Things went silent. Then, the ocean erupted all around them.

The ill-conceived, crude raft, was toppled. Tsiatis and Dytus flew into the ocean. Dytus was consumed by what lay beneath. Tsiatis could hear his death gurgle as he was taken below to suffer what fate the Barrier had in store.

Tsiatis was drawn down into the depths of the ocean, and darkness closed in around him. Mercifully, he lost consciousness before his end came, and the glowing light of his kanalora eyes faded, with one final thought circulating through his mind.

Alas, some secrets are not to be ours in this life.

Originally published in Morpheus Tales #1, July 2008

A Most Unfortunate Gaffe By Aaron A. Polson

"Whatever they bring, you eat it."

Nick Renner swelled in the chest, and glared at Ambassador Jaffe. "Hell, I'll eat just about anything to land this deal. We need the oil rights, and these guys need the legitimacy."

The ambassador, a thin, pale man with a black brushstroke of hair, leaned closer to Renner and whispered again, "Some of the cuisine is just a little, different. But you can't afford to offend Sinaga - the 'chief', got it?"

Renner nodded with a wink.

They sat at the end of a long table of rich, dark wood. Cushions surrounded the table on all sides; the highest ranking of Guntur Sinaga's advisors sat on these pillows, dressed in traditional clothing. All wore head scarves or turbans, sashes of rank, and most had at least a pistol resting in a leather holster at their side. A small mouse of a man wearing no sidearm slipped onto the cushion next to Renner.

"Hello, senator is it? How was your arrival?" the man asked.

Renner glanced at Jaffe. "Fine. Roads are a bit rough. Could probably use some TLC."

"Senator Nicholas Renner, allow me to introduce Pramana Kitishe. He's our contact for Sinaga's organization."

"Please to meet you, Mr. Renner." The small man bowed his head in slow reverence. "Would you mind, what is TLC?"

"Tender-loving-care, looks like-"

"-what the Senator is saying, Pramana," Jaffe interrupted, "is that he thinks Uncle Sam might be able to offer some assistance in the way of infrastructure improvements. Roads, bridges, hospitals, schools. Yes?"

Pramana's lips curled into a little wiry smile. "Ah, yes. The Americans are ever so helpful with their…what is it?" He touched one thin finger to his lips. "Deep pockets."

#

Servants clad in brown hovered like mute bees, ferrying loaded plates to the table, and then empty plates away, with no sound. Guntur Sinaga sat at one end of the table, laughing and talking heartily, but watching Renner with one eye the entire time -

at least Renner felt as though he was stuck and wriggling on Sinaga's pin-hole gaze.

Once the servants floated the last of the dishes from the room, Sinaga motioned for quiet around the table. Pramana stood from his pillow next to Senator Renner, and dutifully hovered to his leader's side. Sinaga was a lined man, his face set with deep, black cracks and rimmed with a hoary beard. When he smiled, his teeth showed in three distinct colourings: a dead brown, stained yellow, and bright gold. He carried the look of someone who had seen much in his life. He motioned Pramana to his side, and the little man obliged.

Pramana nodded and turned to Renner. "Sinaga would like to know what the distinguished gentleman thinks of the dinner thus far?"

At this point, Renner pushed back from the table and pulled at his waist. "Delicious. I must complement the cooks," he said, adding, "and his Excellency for the hospitality." Renner nodded toward Sinaga.

Pramana smiled broadly, "Yes, wonderful. You should know that desert will be even more special. A true... delicacy."

Renner leaned toward the small man. "When can we discuss-"

"Ah," Pramana interrupted, "we will have plenty of time. For now, simply enjoy."

Before the senator from Missouri could respond, the servants returned with covered silver platters. They moved in concert, filing in from the palace kitchens and taking positions around the guests at the table. Each servant slipped his right hand around the handle on his platter's cover, and they snapped these off with a quick and uniform motion.

On each platter, a collection of five large tobacco-hued roaches lay drizzled with a translucent red sauce in the middle of a bed of green leaves. Renner flinched slightly, but returned to a certain stoicism when Jaffe nudged him under the table.

"I'm not eating a god-damn bug," Renner whispered.

Jaffe flushed white. "Please, Nick. This is important."

"I'm not eating that shit." Renner spoke louder this time.

Without calling attention to himself, Pramana slipped from Sinaga's side to the space next to both men. "Gentlemen, is there a problem?"

Renner's face deepened a few shades of red. "Thanks for the offer and all, but I think I'll pass on... um, dessert."

"Sir, this is a fine... delicacy. Our intention is not to offend." Pramana took a slight bow after speaking.

Jaffe leaned closer to the large man and whispered, "C'mon Nick."

Pramana looked at Sinaga, and then back at Renner. "Sir?"

Sinaga's voice sounded, this time in plain, but clear English. "Do you not eat... how is it... decay in your country?"

"He intends the word, mushrooms," Pramana said.

Renner turned to Jaffe. The ambassador nodded, raising his eyebrows. "Well, yes. Where I'm from - well, when I was a boy we'd hunt for Morels, these big mushrooms that would spring up overnight. We'd fill a bag, bring them home, fry them in butter... " His eyes shimmered with the memory.

Sinaga, still unsmiling, said, "In my country, one would not eat the decay - mushrooms. It seems we have some differences in cuisine." He nodded then, like a slight bow - an acknowledgement of his guests, but not necessarily an act of respect.

Pramana watched the old leader for a moment, the room hovering in dense silence. Finally he rose, looked at the Americans, and said, "Simply a cultural misunderstanding. Gentlemen, perhaps we should retire for the evening."

Jaffe paced the floor in Senator Renner's room, a spacious stone cavern lined with beautiful tapestries. Renner, now without his jacket and with his tie hanging loose about his neck, sat on the king-sized bed, leaning forward and resting his elbows on his knees. Both men exchanged a number of nervous looks before one broke the quiet.

"Look, Bill, what did you want me to do? Suck down some prehistoric-sized cockroach just to please a two-bit tribal chief-"

Jaffe stopped in mid-pace, turned to face Renner, and shook his head. "Yes, actually. I thought that was exactly what you planned to do. Remember - 'I'll eat just about anything'?"

Renner's fat fingers pushed through his grey hair. "Hell, that was before the kook's brought me a bug to eat. A god-damn bug. Besides, we smoothed it over, everything will be fine. God, these people are like parasites on this country."

"I hope everything will be fine. Nick, parasites or not, these guys have the power. Whatever you do, make sure not to offend him again. We need-" A sharp knock on the door interrupted Jaffe's words.

Renner quickly held up one hand and mumbled, "Scout's honor" before turning to the door.

Pramana entered, followed by a servant carrying a silver platter. "Mr. Renner, our esteemed leader would like to make amends, so to speak." He snapped at the servant, who promptly brought the platter forward. "I hope you find this a little more to your liking."

Renner and Jaffe exchanged a quick glance. The servant held a tray with small strips of a grey substance that looked like worms doused in a sauce similar to the one from the roaches earlier that evening.

"The senator would be happy to try this." Jaffe nodded at Renner. Pramana remained at the door. "Nick?" Jaffe prodded.

The big man pushed off the bed and approached the tray. He pinched a strip of grey between two fingers, held it for a moment, and slipped it into his mouth. His ruddy face had faded to a faint pink, but the hint of a smile shaded his mouth as his usual colour returned. "Delicious, what is it?"

"Sir, our esteemed leader wants you to feel at home. This is our version of the...how did you say...Morel."

"Well, my compliments. Thank you."

Pramana bowed, snapping once more to the servant, who left the tray on a small table before leaving. Pramana then looked at both men, and said, "I will let our esteemed leader know you are ready to discuss negotiations in the morning," before slipping out after the servant.

Renner woke with a subtle dizziness in the quiet darkness of the confiscated palace. He lurched into a sitting position, and his head swelled and throbbed with the motion. Thoughts tried to form in his brain, but his skull seemed stuffed with foam - light yet dense. Groping for the side of the bed, Renner squirmed onto the floor.

"Bill... " he muttered, calling for Jaffe, "Bill... I... uh!" Renner struck the side of his head with the heel of his hand, trying to knock loose the growing pain. He managed to rest for a minute, doubled over on the floor with his naked feet and hands pressed onto the stone. Usually the cold on his toes would fire a shiver through his body, but Renner began to sweat, convulsing with sharp kicks in his stomach.

He crawled on hands and knees, helpless like a child, toward the heavy wooden door of his room. His fingers caught the edge of the dark wood and crawled up toward the metal latch, but his body convulsed again, and Renner dropped to the stone tiles. After the waves of cramps passed, Renner struggled to his knees, pushed up the latch and pulled the heavy door, dragging it as his body flopped backward.

With the door just open, Renner wrenched through the gap, staggered into the hallway, and stumbled toward Jaffe's room. His mouth tried to form words, but the sounds slowed to muted mumbles in his throat. Renner raised the chapped knuckles of his right hand to rap on the ambassador's door, but another spasm seized his body. He collapsed in a crooked pile on the plush corridor rug.

The big senator from Missouri was finished with pain now. Slowly, almost imperceptibly, the growing fungus began to break through any open orifice in the large man's skull. His eyeballs began to push from their sockets - two wide orbs, like golf balls, thrust from their homes by a yellow-grey foam. The dingy fungus also crept through the man's sinus cavities and through his nostrils, ears, and mouth, like little fingers punching and stretching from any space they could find, to grow up and out. Slowly, over the course of the next few hours, the parasitic fungus devoured most of what made Nicholas Renner - his brain, organs, everything.

###

In the morning, Ambassador William Jaffe opened his bedroom door and gasped. Senator Nick Renner's body, now nothing more than a vessel for the parasitic infestation, lay in a motionless heap on the hallway carpet. The fungus that began its work in the night, now stretched toward the walls and ceiling in long, graceful ribbons of grey. To Jaffe, the whole scene was unreal - just a strange sculpture mocking the Missouri senator with alien adeptness. Jaffe found himself transfixed, locked in some repulsed curiosity, staring at the bizarre corpse.

"Ah, Mr. Jaffe," Pramana called as he walked with deliberate, but casual pace, from the far end of the hall. "Oh, yes. The senator." Pramana shook his head as he closed the last few feet to where Jaffe stood in front of the abomination.

"Good lord..." Jaffe whispered.

"A most unfortunate accident."

Stunned, Jaffe eyed the small man. "Accident?"

"I'm afraid so. Our local mushrooms can be ever-so-dangerous when not prepared properly. Poor Mr. Renner must have fallen victim to an underdone bit of mushroom - I believe you would call this one Cordyceps - one with intact spores. They will, unfortunately, grow quite quickly to a mature fungus, devouring the host from the inside out." Pramana shook his head slightly as he looked at the body and then Jaffe. "This, Mr. Jaffe, is why we rarely eat the mushrooms of our country." His mouth grew into a smile that made Jaffe's skin quiver. "I will report this, make arrangements, and all apologies," he said as he turned to leave. "Oh, and Mr. Jaffe, our esteemed leader says he is ready to discuss matters. Should I tell him the senator is unwell?"

Originally published in Morpheus Tales #1, July 2008

Didn't Remind Me By Robert T. Canipe

My girlfriend Stephanie didn't remind me of a movie star in her looks or personality. She didn't look like Julia Roberts, Will Smith's wife Jada Pickett, or act all affected and flighty like Angelina Jolie. Me, I didn't remind her of Brad Pitt, Denzel Washington, or even Jackie Chan. Stephanie and I were patently unlike anyone else. We weren't together long enough.

When the guy in the ski mask, robbing the busy Larsen's Steak House on a Friday, all-you-can-eat fried flounder for $4.99 night, interrupted our date, grabbed Stephanie from behind and shot her through the left temple because I didn't get my wallet out fast enough to suit him, it didn't remind me of people getting shot in big-budget cop films or even in cheap, made-for-TV movies or series. It didn't remind me of anything. Nope. Nothing at all.

Ski Mask didn't hang around with his two cohorts, Denim Jacket and Baggy Pants, for long after. They didn't fire shots into Larsen's ceiling, warning us not to move for half an hour. They didn't thank anyone. They didn't squeal away in a getaway car. They simply didn't hang around. I didn't see the color of Ski Mask's eyes nor did I notice any distinguishing marks. No one in Larsen's screamed in panic, no one saved the day. Dirty Harry didn't say, "Go ahead. Make my day."

Twenty minutes later, I wasn't eating my rib eye and baked potato (I'm not allergic to fish) but riding not under arrest in the back of a police cruiser, as it didn't closely follow the ambulance. Sirens didn't scream like a banshee nor did we break the speed limit. We didn't run a single, red light. The officer driving didn't glance at me in the cruiser's rearview mirror. He wasn't young and not a little overweight. He didn't really look like a cop. I didn't know what he looked like. His partner in the passenger seat didn't turn around to offer condolences nor did he tell me to be calm that everything would be OK.

At the hospital, it wasn't loud and bustling. No one was running around shouting to start IVs with ringers or get a BP or a blood gas. The ambulance drivers didn't quickly wheel the gurney carrying Steph into a room but moved her slowly behind a curtain and the solitary nurse didn't let me come along. I sat down in a leather, wingback chair that didn't look like it belonged there. Five or six doctors didn't run behind the curtain to join the nurse but only one. I couldn't see his and the nurse's silhouettes on the curtain, as they didn't fiddle with Stephanie. I couldn't tell what they were doing, but it wasn't at all like they do things on ER.

Later, the doctor, a not-so-middle-aged man with a head of black, curly toupee didn't come out and tell me Stephanie wasn't dead. She'd expired. I started to ask him if that wasn't like what a parking meter or a library card does, but I bit back the curt rejoinder, didn't glance at his nametag, didn't smile. He didn't smile either and didn't speak up, muttering something else which I didn't hear as the farmer/cop was not looking at me again but talking at me, asking me if he couldn't call someone.

The funeral wasn't like the ones I'd seen in the movies. It wasn't sadder, or bleaker, nor did it have good dialogue. None of the participants acted as they should. Had there been a director, he'd have not yelled "Action!" The writing didn't work. The casting was all wrong.

Stephanie wasn't on view. I'd complained that the stainless steel coffin wasn't open. The scene looked quite unlike those that I'd seen on HBO and in films. The undertaker hadn't corrected me when I called it a coffin. Coffins aren't four-sided. Caskets aren't contoured with the six sides. Caskets aren't like the ones the Dodge City undertaker builds in John Wayne and Clint Eastwood films. The undertaker didn't tell me they didn't call him an undertaker anymore. He didn't tell me what they call him.

The undertaker said that the casket wasn't open because Ski Mask's .357 bullet hadn't left Stephanie's skull in good shape. He couldn't fix it. I'd never thought these guys were anything but artists and couldn't not make anybody look natural. I didn't tell the guy this. "We're not miracle workers," he moaned. "We can't make violence pretty." I didn't nod, trying not to remember the look on Steph's face that night at Larsen's Steak House as the bullet plowed into her brain. She hadn't pleaded for her life. She didn't cry. She hadn't looked afraid. For a second, she'd looked unconventional, as if she'd misremembered something vastly unimportant. Her eyes didn't roll up, although one of them - the left one, I think - didn't remain in its socket.

Ski Mask didn't lay her gently to the floor then, didn't scream at me to remember what he'd told me about not being slow in giving him all my money, credit cards, hell, the whole, damn wallet. I don't remember handing it to him. I couldn't remember any blood either, although my mom said the stains on the sport coat I no longer wear were never coming out. I never wore nor looked at the coat again.

Steph's dad Ray bought her casket. It wasn't the cheapest, he'd said. It wasn't what she deserved. Stephanie never got what she deserved, her mom Rachel didn't declare but her not looking at me said it loudly. Rachel and Ray'd never liked me much; Ray'd once told me that I wasn't what he'd envisioned his daughter settling down with. He'd never said what that vision was. After the funeral, we didn't keep in touch. Neither he nor Rachel had reminded me at the cemetery to come and see them. We weren't from the same side of the tracks.

My parents didn't come. They'd never liked that Steph was not white (not African-American; Steph didn't like hyphens; she said she was only Stephanie, she just wasn't pink, don't colour me!). My parents had never tried to get along with Ray or Rachel. My mom didn't call, didn't say that those people are nothing but inherently violent, have nothing but violence in their genes. Ski Mask didn't have black hands, the one that held the gun wasn't black, wasn't coloured at all. It didn't remind me of anything.

Nothing in our apartment reminds me of Stephanie. I don't know why. It doesn't seem like a different place. For some reason, there is no grief attached to any of the knick-knacks we shared. I don't yet miss her. There is no grief. I'd not searched for it since she died just to satisfy everyone with tears at the funeral. I didn't know if I could find it.

Dr. Pearson said don't look for the grief. He said that I'm in shock. I don't know. Having never been in shock, I have to believe him. He told me these things as I sat on a chair in a very bright room in an office decorated with autographed baseball memorabilia. It was not at all like any psychiatrist office I'd ever seen on TV. Dr. Pearson himself was a buff, athletic-looking man, not at all like the balding, stuttering shrink on the Bob Newhart Show. My insurance was paying $100 an hour for him to find out why I don't feel, and he spends half of every session doing a monologue talking about the Braves not winning and their terrible, unwatchable pitching staff.

He asked me if I was never going back to Larsen's. I hadn't thought about it, I said. I'd never been there in my life before that night. It wasn't cheap, and the food wasn't that good. I'd not balked at going there because Steph had wanted to. She'd had something special to tell me. She'd said that she wanted a special place to tell it. I think she was trying to be dramatic. Stephanie liked those type movies.

"What was it that she told you?" Pearson asked. "Can you remember?"

"No," I said. "She never got a chance to. Ski Mask didn't let her."

"What do you think it was she couldn't tell you until you were at the steak house?"

I shrugged. "Don't know. If it were a movie, I'd reckon she wasn't planning to stay with me. They don't tell you things like that in private, but find a crowded place where you won't make a scene."

"But that wasn't - this isn't - the movies," he said.

"No," I said. "It isn't. The blood isn't the right color. The shots don't sound right. There's no echo." I'd never thought about that before.

He didn't say anything.

My insurance didn't pay but for two more sessions. I wasn't upset. I didn't like baseball.

They never caught the three guys. There was never a trial, never any media parked outside my house asking for interviews, never any real closure. Neither Wolf Blitzer on CNN nor Bill O'Reilly on Fox did a story. Greta Van Susteren never called. The cops had no leads. They didn't assign a team of detectives to the case, didn't invite the FBI. Clarice Starling never arrived. I didn't complain. Didn't they have cold case teams for unsolved cases? Wouldn't they find new evidence?

I never ran into Ski Mask, nor Denim Jacket, nor Baggy Pants in line at the Burger King, the drycleaners, or at the video store, nor did I spot them on TV running for political office, selling used cars, or preaching. I never hunted them down like in the comic books or the paperback thrillers. I was neither the Punisher nor the Executioner. They never robbed or even killed again. At least not in this town, nor in the places I no longer go.

I haven't been back to work for while. I don't speak to anyone in the park or in the bookstore. Last Sunday at the park, I didn't ask the woman with the brightly-coloured, expensive baby stroller whether the infant curled up and asleep inside was or wasn't a girl or a boy. I neither asked about her swelling belly nor about the sex of the foetus curled up and asleep inside of it. The glow surrounding her didn't remind me of anything. I didn't want to think about what she'd look like shot through the head, one eye blown out.

I never found out what Stephanie didn't tell me. I don't ask her parents, or the cops, or the doctors if they know or if they don't. I don't go to church, don't fall down on the altar, don't scream at God and ask "Why me Lord? What have I ever done?" like Kris Kristofferson. I don't talk to ministers, priests, or television evangelists on the phone or Internet. I don't consult psychics, the stars like in the Zodiac, or stars like Tom Cruise. I don't join Scientology, grief counselling, or support groups. I don't seek answers. I don't ask questions. I don't like being reminded.

Sometimes I do think about asking Stephanie herself. Or God.

But neither of them is talking.

Originally published in Morpheus Tales #2, October 2008

Paper Wasp And Chocolate Rabbits By Mari Mitchell

With her bony hip, Martha Knox pushed open the door to her house. Her hands were full. In one, her collection of keys, in the other, a small plastic-wrapped item that appeared to be furry, and bloody. She placed it on the counter. Her housemate Elsa was on the phone talking, while she sipped a cup of coffee.

"Hold on for a moment, Laura." She put down her cup, and pushed the hold button on her phone. "That better not be what I think it is."

"Which is?" Martha replied as her khaki backpack slid off her small shoulders and onto the kitchen floor. The pack, heavy with her college textbooks made a thud as it hit the white tile floor. Requiring a M.D. to become a pathologist meant a great deal of studying.

"A dead squirrel," Elsa replied.

"Wrong! It's a mort sylvilagus bachmani."

Disgusted, she poured her coffee down the drain and followed Martha with the cordless phone. She spoke into the phone, "I'm going to have to call you back in a little while sweetheart. I've got to kill Martha and clean another of her messes. Bye."

By now, Martha was pouring coffee into a huge cup filled halfway with ice and cream.

"A dead rabbit! We have an agreement. You swore that none of your "projects" would EVER come into the kitchen area. Why didn't you go around the back and straight into your room with it?"

She held up her cup. "I needed coffee."

Elsa reached into a drawer and put on disposable gloves. "You need a huge kick in the ass, that's what you need! Then you need to go to a doctor and get a prescription for whatever the hell is wrong with you!" From under the sink she took out a spray bottle that contained bleach. She started to run hot water into it as well.

"Nahhh. I just needed a quick fight with you before you left for the weekend." She smiled a wicked twinkle in her eyes.

"You're going to make all of us sick with this disgusting hobby of yours. You would think anyone in Mensa and years of college would know better."

Martha picked up the small carcass, "The odds of catching something from an animal are not that great. Why would I do it if I felt there was a real chance of becoming ill?"

"Because you like to press people's buttons. It's one of your ways of getting attention. And because you need pills! Lots of them, in all sorts of colors and shapes."

"Now what would Tom Cruise say about that?"

Martha was in the hall that led to her part of the house, Elsa scurrying behind her with the spray bottle.

"Need I remind you that there hasn't been a reported case of francisella tularensis or myxomatosis in this area for over two years?" Martha said emphatically.

"Need I remind you that when you're dead it doesn't matter?"

Martha mockingly pantomimed licking the dead rabbit, then slammed her door.

"EUWWW! You don't only need pills, but you do need a fucking STRAIGHTJACKET and then maybe a nice LOBOTOMY! I'll bring the ice pick."

Elsa washed the kitchen surfaces and the floors with the bleach solution. She even washed the walls of the hall and Martha's door. When she was through, Elsa knocked on the door to Martha's room, hoping to be heard over the awful EMO music that was blaring form the speakers. Elsa said in a small voice, "I liked you better when we were kids." She pushed the door open cautiously. "Mar, Martha." Now in the room, she could tell that her housemate of the last three years was in the shower. She reached over to turn off the CD and eased the bathroom door open part way. "Hey Doctor Frankenstein, Laura and I are leaving for our trip in a few minutes. I am sorry about what I said." This, she said half-heartedly. "I'm leaving the info on the fridge. We should be back Tuesday evening around eight or so. Okay? I'll bring you back a present. Want anything special?"

The water turned off and Elsa handed her the pink towel that was lying on the sink. "Well, Igor, or should I say Igoress? How about a stuffed rabbit?"

With a pretend lisp Elsa said, "Yeth mathter."

A car horn beeped in three short, happy bursts. "Laura's here. Got to go."

It was on her way out that she saw the table with the plastic over it. Something lumpy was covered on top of it. She was sure it was a freshly dissected road-killed-rabbit.

On the drive to Napa, Elsa vented to Laura.

"Well I think Martha's off her stool and on the floor of madness."

"Now Laura, she's not that bad. It's not like she's killing things. They're already dead. She says that there is beauty in every organ, poetry in bones and wonderment in the sinews. To understand the components of life is to understand what makes it possible."

"It's creepy. What if one day she contracts a brain disease and kills you in your sleep?"

"That's not going to happen."

"How do you know?"

"Because that kind of thing only happens in bad movies and this is real life."

"How can I argue with that kind of logic? Let's drop it and enjoy the trip."

"Fine with me." Laura caressed Elsa's hand.

Martha cleared the remains of the rabbit away and briefly rinsed her hands. She made a quick sandwich and plunked down to do some studying. There was no getting around it; Russian Literature was boring. She put the thick book down and said to the empty room, "This should have been called War and Snore."

Martha felt tired and a little achy. It was only nine o'clock but it seemed so much later. She reasoned that if she went to bed a little early she could wake-up even earlier. No good would come from forcing herself to stay awake. Martha knew herself well enough to know nothing she studied would stick.

In her room, she snuggled underneath the harlequin quilt. Once asleep, wild Technicolor fevered dreams consumed her. Mixtures of movies and real life erupted making it hard for her to tell where one began and the other ended.

Martha knew she was at home but somehow she was also in the Sahara Desert. It was bright - brighter than mid-day on the summer solstice. She turned on the shower and collapsed to the floor. At first the water felt hot but she did not feel as if she could find the energy to care. Her brown eyes had become thick and heavy like lead sheets closed. Rain. The drought of the desert was over. Baked earth and skin drank the water in. Far away, a ringing echoed. She tried to ignore the sound but the more she tried the louder it became. She turned her head; a yellow origami wasp appeared and dipped its stinger into a cup of tea. "She must be a paper wasp."

"Martha get up. We have shopping to do."

"I want some tea too," she said with her mouth and throat dry as hot sand.

The wasp paid no attention, but put three more sugar cubes into its tea. Like most insects, it was partial to sweet things.

"Mar come on." The words floated in the air like purple smoke. She reached up with one hand and touched the "n" making it dissipate into butterflies. She laughed. Periwinkle smoked words came, "Re... dick... u... lesssss."

"What's ridiculous is laying there like road kill.." Now the words altered in colour and vibrancy. She followed the trail of cotton candy words out of the shower and into the kitchen.

"Elsa, I don't feel... right."

"That's because you're leftovers." A huge brush cottontail stood holding a spray bottle in its paws.

She stared at the rabbit. "I'm sorry, have we met before?"

"I should say so." He turned and faced her. His abdomen was open and hollow. The spinal column could clearly be seen; glistening crimson and pink tissue clung to ribs.

Her brown eyes glazed over as Martha gave a small nodding of her head in agreement. "Oh."

"Are you ready?"

Martha scanned the room looking for a sign of what to do next. From her hall, that ringing-buzzing came again. The sound was not distant this time. It was so loud she wondered how the hollow rabbit could hear her. The thought then occurred to her: of course he could, rabbits have great hearing with their long ears.

A long piece of paper unravelled like a New Year's party favour, blowing raspberries, at her, with its forked tongue. Now Maratha was wishing she had taken some Nyquil before she went to bed. It would have saved her from talking to animals.

The rabbit was speaking, "Large garbage bags, and a small hand saw. Mar hurry! Or the jackets will get in."

Something was batting the windows. Their faces appeared as if they were made of white wax. No features could be discerned. The long arms of the straightjacket batted at the glass, like strange demented moths trying to touch the light.

She was in a different place now, one filled with dark molasses. "What did he say?"

The wasp hovered behind her still; the stinger flicked at Martha as a bead of fuchsia liquid pooled at its tip. There was something familiar about that wasp but she couldn't make the connections.

A choir of song began. She turned around to see where the music was coming from. A shaft of light shone on the small Makita handsaw. She picked it up and made her way out of the pool of molasses. When she was almost free of the dark stickiness, the wasp woman handed her three wooden dowels. Martha recognized them as the sticks that used to be in her birdcage. She held them up to her chest and considered them carefully. "These should do fine."

Martha placed the things on her desk, which was pushed up, beside her bed. A long tether pulled her out of the room and back into the kitchen.. With clown's feet, she trudged through.

"You have more things to gather."

"Do you smell chocolate?" The rabbit-of-hollow no longer had its speckled grey fur. Now instead of soft rabbit fur he was smooth and light brown in colour. The undead-rabbit sat in a field of Easter grass. His ears gone, nibbled away by the wasp.

"Poor bunny."

She positioned the pots around the bed and covered the duvet with trash bags.

As Martha lay down she said, "Won't this be fun!" The wasp and rabbit readily agreed.

"Poetry to uncover. Beauty to unveil. Wonderment to discover." The hollow chocolate rabbit said as he began to melt.

"It won't hurt will it?"

"Has it ever hurt before?"

Martha shook her head; no.

"Why would it now?"

Another Martha appeared in the room dressed in surgical greens. "You're right, dead-rabbit."

The room filled with music. Though she did not recognize the song she tried to sing along anyway. The wasp woman sprayed Martha's chest with hot bleach.

Both Marthas said as one, "Thank you."

The Martha in green gave a quick but messy "Y" cut on the torso of the naked Martha with a scalpel. "That's better. Be-careful, we wouldn't want to make a mess for Elsa to clean up."

Martha giggled like an impish child. "No we wouldn't want that."

She pulled the skin away, revealing muscles, bones and organs.

Martha in green picked up the cordless handsaw. At only four pounds it was easy to handle. With her left hand she felt for the xyphoid process of the other Martha and pressed the blade under it. The four-inch blade began to whirl. It tore through flesh but had a more difficult time with the sternum. With a little perseverance and pressure, the handsaw did its job. Tissue, once whole, spilt and then became a moat filled with blood.

Like French doors opening to a Garden of Eden, the ribcage expanded out. They said in a joint pink whisper. "Breathtaking." Wooden dowels kept the bones from closing. Ribbons of large and small intestine were placed in pots.

"Oh dear," the standing Martha said, her surgical greens now black, her figure fading into bloody shadows, "I'd so hoped to see our heart before we ran out of blood."

"I'm home Martha," Elsa called out as she put her bags down on the kitchen floor. "What the hell happened here?" She looked around the once neat kitchen. It looked as if elephants had come to tea. Pots and pans were scattered everywhere. The refrigerator door was open. The smell of rotting food thick in the air. Panic filled her mind. Something was wrong.

She gave a quick look to see if she saw any blood or a sign of the break in and saw none. "Mar, are you all right?" Elsa headed towards Martha's wing of the house. Opening the door causally, hoping to find her asleep with her head phones on like she had so many times before.

An intense pungent odour assaulted her nostrils with a distinctive smell - a smell of decaying death. The image that presented itself would forever linger in the shadows of her mind. Peaceful dreamscapes would morph to nightmares.

Originally published in Morpheus Tales #2, October 2008

Cicadas By Nickolas Cook

Willa felt a hysterical sob building at the back of her chest and she flung the rest of the wet clothes back in the basket. Hands shaking, she snatched up the clean laundry and dashed back into the ramshackle house, stumbled into the sweaty-hot kitchen, and threw herself into a chair. She mashed her hands against her ears, and felt the frustrated tears roll down her cheeks.

They screeched on and on…so much, so loudly that Willa Jackson could hardly stand it anymore. A few days before, when the cicadas had first begun to flit through the hazy, humid summer air, their buzzing numbers had delighted and astounded her. All those tiny black bodies darting like acrobatic bullets in the drooping trees, ticking into the strangle of the tall summer grass, made the world seem alive with motion. She had shared their excitement, being that it was summer and she out of school for a couple of months. But when the mating males began that high pitched, almost tear-inducing 'screeeeeeeeeee - screeeeeeeeeee-screeeeeeeeeee' it had been like a sudden slap in the face. The unrelenting noise had expunged her joy, and had become a constant drip-drip of water on her consciousness, pick-pick-picking away at her nerves, until she finally could take it no more.

Mama came to her, forced her hands down, her gaze a mix of concern and amusement. "Your first time, child. Lord knows they can sure get on a body's nerves. Always there, buzzin' away." Mama shifted her ponderous weight into the chair across from her daughter and started to shell black-eyed peas for dinner. She scooped a handful of them from the steel pot and placed them before the sobbing teenager. "You just got to keep your mind occupied with something else until you get used to 'em."

"I can't… I can't… "

"Shhh… hush that up now. You can take it. They ain't goin' away just cause you don't like 'em." Willa heard the edge to her mother's voice. Sullenly, she wiped away her tears and reached for the peas. Her fingers dug at the soft husk without thought, dumped the peas into the pot.

After a few minutes of hearing the girl sniffle, Mama shook her head. "We gonna need some fatback for the peas. Why don't you walk down to Mingus's and get some?"

Willa nodded, wiping at her runny nose. Mama mined her housecoat pockets and drew out a small wad of carefully hoarded dollar bills. Counting off two, she handed them over. Willa took them, but held her head down so Mama would not see the small smile creep across her mouth. Mingus's was her favorite place to be. Being the only grocery for ten miles in any direction, for the poor folk of the tiny hamlet of Hillsborough, Georgia, it was about the only place to be. Usually Mama didn't let her walk to the store alone. Too many eyes, was her enigmatic response. Too many eyes watching you get bigger in all the wrong places, girl.

Willa hurried out the door before Mama could change her mind.

"Don't slam the door, child," Mama called after her, but Willa was already running along the shaded dirt road, her lean dark form cutting through the shadows and ambient 'screeeeeeeeeee-screeeeeeeeeee-screeeeeeeeeee' of singing cicadas like a stone dropped into deep water.

The road coiled past open fields of grass on both sides, separated by Old Man Honey's rickety wooden fence. A peck of crows sat on the leaning posts and watched her with belligerent coal-black eyes as she hurried by. One massive dark bird clutched a cicada in its talons; it gazed at her as it slowly dissected the struggling insect.

It was a four-mile walk to Mingus's, but for Willa the journey was far from tedious. She had grown up in these woods, so even the trees that bordered the rough path were like old friends. Some of them were older than the oldest person in Hillsborough, and the woods held their secrets well. She felt like nothing more than an eye blink to the ancient woods steady progress. Their nearest neighbor was Charity Rose, a woman who seemed to the young girl to be as old as the trees, and her house sat a little off the road, tucked into a sleepy corner of willow and oak shadows; a faded white fence directed the old woman's infrequent visitors up the dirt path to her old tin shack.

Rounding the curve Willa saw a stranger leaning on the fence as she approached, a narrow man, holding a beat up guitar across his chest. His white smile razor cut along his sensuous lips. His cheekbones were obsidian rock chiseled from the black hardness of his skin, his hands, lean wire and bone, stitched together by night. Perfect moon nails glittered in the lazy afternoon sun. His eyes reminded her of the crows, but there was something about his glance that sent a strange shiver through her suddenly quivering frame. The cicadas rose in crescendo, as the man moved forward to intercept her wary approach, and then died down to a low brain-tickling drone.

Who was this stranger? She wondered. Kin folk of Mrs. Rose?

She didn't think she liked the way he kept staring at her. Not mostly.

"Slow down, little girl," he said. His fingers began to idly pick at the guitar strings, pulling strange notes from them. "Where you off to on such a hot day? Why don't ya sit a while and talk with a lonely traveler?"

Willa edged away from him. Her eyes darted towards Mrs. Rose's porch in the hopes of seeing the old woman, but the house was closed up and silent. Strange that she would have the doors and windows closed up on such a hot day. Maybe the cicada sound had driven her to put up with the stifling heat.

"What's wrong, little one?" he asked. "Cat got your tongue?" The strange man's smile grew more luminescent with every passing moment. He moved closer and closer to Willa, eyes narrowed, hands flexing on the neck of the guitar as if he would choke the song from it. "Sure do look sweet, don't you? So fresh and smooth. My goodness, yes. You got a face like a little angel, girl. Come on over here and let me touch those cheeks, baby girl."

She felt her heart triple beat, a counterpoint to the thrum of the blood-shudder in her veins, and the whirr of the unseen insects. Her stare flicked past him again at the old woman's shut up house. Curiosity turned to a kind of vague transcendent morbidity and she grew more afraid of this strange man and his terrible leering smile.

He sensed her apprehension. "Don't worry about that old woman," he said with a shake of his wooly head. "You too young to worry so much. Come on over here and sit with me on her porch for spell. Maybe I can show you a trick or two on this here guitar." He held it up to her, as if to prove his feigned harmlessness.

"I-I got to go, mister," Willa murmured. "Mama'll beat me for sure if I don't hurry." She felt her face grow warm with the hasty excuse, but deep down she sensed something dark wafting from this man, a spiritual negation that made her feel bone cold even in the sultry heat. It was a sensation both terrifying and compelling. She wanted to touch his skin. Would it be icy? Would it feel as smooth as coal? And those eyes flashed like lightning bugs in the depth of his face...

He moved a few feet closer; his fingers stopped their indolent picking. His smile and eyes tried to pinion her fast to the spot.

The cicada monotonic rose again, ripping across her consciousness, releasing her from the man's hypnotic stare.

"Got to go... "

And she dashed away like a frightened gazelle, bare feet digging into the dirt road. Behind her, his laughter rose on an upsurge of cicada buzzing.

By the time she reached Mingus's, her body was trembling with a mixture of exhaustion and excitement. She slowed a few hundred yards from the cul-de-sac where the store squatted. The single gas pump, old tires stacked in leaning heaps to the side, and gathering of old men on the front porch were as familiar and comforting to her as home. She felt more than a little silly now about her fear of the stranger. Maybe he was a lonely man, a traveler, as he claimed, and she had callously turned from his need. Bible said to love your neighbor, to comfort those in need, like Jesus would have done. Now she felt ashamed too. Mostly she didn't like the way he had made her feel when he looked at her. Her skin tingled with the remembrance even now.

She climbed the creaking steps of the porch and the old men (many of them not so old as she imagined) stopped their gabbing to watch her ascend. She knew most of them. Or at least they knew mama and daddy. One toothless man she didn't know toasted her with a brown bag wrapped drink. "How ya' doin', honey? Hot day, ain't it?"

She nodded, but kept her eyes on the store's screen door ahead.

One of the men, Mr. Johnson, gave the old man a frown and shook his head. "How you're Mama doin', Willa?" he asked, sipping from a bottle of coke.

"She's okay, Mister Johnson." Willa tried not to feel their eyes crawling over her bare legs and shoulders. Some didn't bother to hide their frank gaze at her developing chest.

"Well, you tell her I said 'hello', okay?"

"Yes, sir."

She hurried inside the store on the tail end of the amused chirp of the men's chuckles. She waited for her eyes to adjust to the murk, and then began to move down the aisles, picking up new combs and hair ribbons, admiring the crimson spill of silk and the soft night of the black velvet. She looked with envy at the explosions of colors safely trapped inside the candy jars: sweets and gums and salty delights. But, like the ribbons, Mama had told her time and again they didn't have money for such things.

She hung her head and made her way to the butcher counter. A large woman in a blue housedress was talking with the butcher, a smallish gray haired old man. "Damn these god awful cicadas," she bawled, rolling her enormous brown eyes. "They about to drive us crazy at home, clinging to the windows and flying into the food if we leave the door open for a minute. Glad they only come every thirteen years. They'd drive me to drink if they come any more than that." She ended her pronouncement with a harsh snort of laughter.

The butcher chuckled and shook his head. "I hear ya' now. I found one of the little bastards in my milk last night. Bout lost my dinner. Least they don't hang around once they's done matin'. We got that to be thankful for."

A short man in coveralls sidled up to the counter and leaned his rotund weight against the wooden case. His dire tone knifed through the laughter. "They's another reason to hate 'em, you know."

The butcher's smile fell away. "Sure enough heard that. Never did catch him, did they?"

"Maybe this time he won't come round," the woman said. "Maybe he done found somewhere else to go. Maybe he dead."

The leaning man nodded, as if seriously considering the possibility. "Might be... I don't believe he gonna die so easy though. I know folks last time wondered if he was human at all. Started callin' him the Cicada Man, didn't they?"

The butcher chopped a furry leg from a concealed dead animal. "Sure did. And that's a right enough name for him. Come round, do his thing, and then gone when the little bastards leave again. Regular as clockwork."

The leaning man dug at a tooth with a dirty fingernail. "Thirteen years don't seem long enough right about now, does it?"

"That poor girl." The large woman shook her head. "Wasn't even a full grown girl yet."

"Wasn't no older than fourteen," said the butcher. "Her parents never were the same after that. General started drinkin' and never stopped. His wife just up and left. Nobody never heard from her again."

The woman rolled her large eyes again. "Well, they might have kept that girl a little more dressed. Don't do for men to see that kind of thing, even in one so young as fourteen. Some men ain't got no lick of sense when it comes to young girls. Some men-" The butcher saw Willa and gave the woman a small shake of his head. She turned on her with a cross frown, as if the girl had purposely snuck up on her.

"What can I get for you, Willa?" asked the butcher.

"Here another one," the woman muttered, giving the leaning man a meaningful eye roll.

Shame burned Willa's cheeks. Once again she felt the exposed flesh of her naked legs and shoulders, the loose weight of her budding breasts pushing against her thin shirt, and knew where the comment had been aimed. She kept her eyes on the floor, not daring to challenge the older woman's disapproval.

The fat back purchased (tied up in a greasy brown bag by the butcher) she hurried past the roving eyes of the men on the porch, and trotted back down the dirt road towards home. A mile before Mrs. Rose's house she stopped to catch her breath. Part of her wanted to stroll past it to see if the man was still there. If she found him there again, strumming his old guitar, smiling that big smile of his, she would make herself be nice for him, even if he scared her. She would sit with him on the porch swing and talk about his travels.

But another part of her, a part that had a voice very much like Mama's, said that tempting the devil was dangerous. And why was Mrs. Rose's house all closed up on a hot day like this? That man was no good. You could see it in his eyes, could sense it in his body. Those thin fingers could too easily snag, tear, pull apart delicate places, without care or delicacy... they could...

Willa's legs trembled at the thought of his touch in those secret places.

She made up her mind. Head held high, she continued along the road, determined to show the stranger some sort of kindness, but when she reached Mrs. Rose's house the porch was empty. The temptation to go knock on the door was strong, but a dark blossom of doubt and fear of what she might find inside (maybe old Mrs. Rose laid open like a side of meat, all of her secret places exposed) decided her against it. Instead, she gripped the fatback tighter and headed home.

Later that day, in the kitchen, she said nothing to her mother about the man with the guitar, but instead asked about the Cicada Man. Mama paused in her dissection of the fatback into the pot of beans. "Where you hear about that nonsense, child?"

"Down to the store."

"Well, you don't pay that any attention," she said. "We ain't gonna let nobody hurt you."

"What'd he do, Mama?"

"Ain't nothin' you need to worry about," Mama said as she sliced the last of the thick slab of greasy meat.

"He hurt some girl a long time ago?"

"I said you ain't got to worry about it. You was just a baby when that happened. Ain't nothin' like that ever gonna happen to you, cause I'm gonna protect you from all the Cicada Mens in the world. Now go wash up so you can help me make some biscuits, girl."

At the water pump she found the ethereal skeleton of a cicada. Every ridge and bulge of its body had been left behind and seemed in the rays of the slowly setting sun to be rarified. She plucked it from the pump handle as if it were a jewel and cradled the gauzy casement in her palm. The blankness of the round eyes reminded her of the crows this afternoon, which in turn drove her thoughts to the man again. She remembered his smooth dark skin, lean fingers, his white smile, those perfect teeth, like a hungry dog...

In the forest the cicada noise rose again, slicing through the early evening air, and her hand involuntarily snapped closed. Willa whirled around and stared hard at the gathering of shadows where the pines met behind their house, trying to make sense of the twilight shiftings. But the shadows held their secrets and she didn't dare to move closer to peel them back. She opened her fingers. The cicada shell had been crushed. Its ridges and bulges were nothing more than wispy fuscous fragments now.

And still the cicadas' mating 'screeeeeeeeeee-screeeeeeeeeee-screeeeeeeeeee' continued.

Willa went to bed that night, grateful to find sanctuary in the darkness of her room. The heat was stifling and sweat was already beginning to roll down her chest. She ratcheted open her window and lay on the bed she had been steadily outgrowing for the last two years. She thought about the man again, and wondered where he'd sleep tonight, did he find food today, had someone feed him like a good Christian should? But soon her thoughts fell from such Christian ponderings and she wondered how his skin would feel, smooth and black as night. She saw his hands, his sinewy fingers, plucking and pulling at the resistant guitar strings. The cicada drone stuck to the surface of her thoughts like the not too intrusive black spots when one looks too long at the sun, and the 'screeeeeeeee' followed her into sleep.

What woke her later?

The rising swell of the cicadas' mating song?

Or was it the soft pluck-pluck of the guitar in the woods?

Willa's heart skipped a beat.

Had she dreamed the sound?

Sweat rolled down between her breasts. Her breath stuck in her throat, she strained her ears to tear through the noise of the cicadas for the insinuating strum of guitar strings. She peered into the moonlit night beyond her screened window, but nothing moved.

Then she heard it again and her blood chilled in her veins.

The guitar. The man was here. In the woods behind the house.

Willa grabbed a shirt and pants and dressed with the light off. Making her way past her parents' room, steps light on the creaking boards of the old house, her breath quivered like a bird in her throat. The evening was cool enough to prickle her exposed flesh; goose pimples rose and her nipples hardened. The moon showered the night world in dappled silver. Shadows stood guard in the pines as she moved closer to the stand of trees. Nothing felt real except the cold beat of her heart, the quicksilver pulse of her veins.

"Hey, girl," the voice whispered from the pines. "You sure look sweet as a peach. Come on in here and let's talk for a spell."

The soft voice of the guitar sang in the darkness. Two beetle carapace eyes shined from the deep shadows.

The cicada drone escalated to painful proportions.

Willa stepped beyond the moonlight. As the breath of night kissed her naked skin, long, thin fingers reached from the murk to embrace her.

And the song rose and rose... 'screeeeeeeeeee—-screeeeeeeeee-screeeeeeeeeee'

Originally published in Morpheus Tales #2, October 2008

Bloody Kisses: Tragedy By Christian McPhate

Black candles burned low in the room, illuminating the red silk curtains framing the stone window. Shattered wine glasses were scattered across the floor, droppings of blood staining the jagged pieces. Soft moans filled the shadowed atmosphere as my lover responded to the light kisses that I placed upon her neck, caressing her skin with my blood red tongue, images of our meeting flashing through my mind, screams of her denial echoing in my ears.

I, of course, should have expected no less from her, for I had found her in the trash-strewn alleys of the city and mistook her for one of my kind; after all, she did have the teeth.

But her sparkling red blood proved my assumptions of her vampiric heritage wrong when I slit her wrist to fill her wine glass; she nearly woke the dead with her screams.

It had been such a long time since I last visited with one of my own kind. We are such solitary creatures, to say the least, and there was a certain level of immaturity within the immortal community that the cattle rarely achieved during their pathetically short lives.

After breaking more than a few vampire protocols with my seduction, I swayed her to the rational side of thinking. I assure you that it was unintentional, and I was merely trying to quiet her screams. Normally, I would not waste my time on her type of cattle, but I was hungry and my particular delicacies were not easy to find in this ancient American city.

Randal constantly formulated conspiracy theories, attempting to explain the shortage of food: a vampiric governmental agency manipulating the cattle with powers far beyond my imagination, for example.

Alas, my assistant was a little crazy.

As I massaged my lover's jugular vein, she pressed her naked body against mine, powerless against my power. Before I could finish my meal, however, a loud knock echoed through my bedchamber.

"My dear, I apologize for this interruption, but I shall return."

Her head tilted slightly, revealing a luscious neck tattooed with my bloody kisses, and I rose off my dying lover while she stared at me with beautiful sightless eyes.

I smoothed the wrinkles out of my black cape and turned to face my child as he stepped through the doorway, interrupting my feeding once again. Straightening the collar of my white shirt, I approached him with an air of nobility unknown in this particular age.

"Edward," I hissed, red eyes blazing with fire, "why must you persist in bothering me when I have a guest for a nightcap?"

He lowered his eyes, avoiding my gaze, and whispered, "Umm... well... um, you seem to get all the damn women, and I'm left to feed on the servants!"

I glanced at my lover as she exhaled her last breath.

"Yes, she was fulfilling," I replied, "but it is not my fault that you must feed on the hired help, for it is the rule of dead; after all, it takes many centuries to reach my level of power."

Edward crossed his arms and began tapping his foot, tiring of hearing the same explanation, time after time. And from the look on his face, he seemed to be entertaining thoughts that I had not entertained since the slaying of my master several centuries prior to my reawakening.

"Besides," I whispered, "it is not my fault that women find me irresistible."

"You're a stubborn ass and I'm-"

My child stopped and stared at me with widened eyes. He stuttered a couple of more times, but I ignored his gasping complaints and slowly walked toward the open window, to stare at the full moon moving slowly across the night sky.

As I washed my soul in the radiant light of my mother's orb, my child's body hit the ebony floor of my temporary keep.

"Thank you, Randal," I said, turning to face my dearest (but often times annoying) assistant.

Randal scratched his head with a bloody stake; the sight of the life nectar nearly drove me insane with hunger. Then he reached behind his back, with an evil glint in his eyes, and revealed a rather large machete. He raised the blade, his feeble arms shaking, and beheaded my child.

"Randal," I whispered, turning away from the grizzly scene, "shall we go for another drive?"

#

The darkness of the mechanical carriage comforted my soul, soothing the bothersome images of my past. The city was alive tonight. Prostitutes stood on the trash-filled corners of the streets, displaying their goods and tantalizing the eyes of the night with their rather large breasts. Although I was hungry, their drug-infested veins held no particular place in my dark heart.

Strewn about the streets like human garbage left out to rot, hundreds of homeless people milled through the alleyways like desolate souls discarded by society. A knightly bum dressed in the tattered wears of a golfer strode through a crowd of hookers, pimps, and panhandlers. His plaid pants were torn and ragged, and he displayed a broken tennis racket similar to King Arthur carrying the fabled Excalibur, parting the sea of deviants akin to the prophet Moses parting the Red Sea.

Ah, the blackness of the night called to my soul, signing a song of death and destruction, a symphony of fear that echoed throughout the mechanical carriage. Tiny pinpricks of lights glowed through the shroud of darkness, marring its beauty as the fire of the street lamps flashed by the window like a continuous stream of light.

As my mother's light parted the clouds above the city, my thoughts drifted back to my awakening. I was relieved to find that humanity had flourished into a new age of science and technology, stepping away from the dark ages of religious belief.

"Christ," mumbled my assistant, dropping his flask of whiskey.

Then, to my surprise, a brilliant illumination, brighter than the noontime sun, slammed into the side of the mechanical carriage. Dark-tinted glass shattered, broken shards piercing my cold flesh.

Although I was already dead, the same could not be said for my assistant. As the weight of the car pressed against my chest, I wondered if the old bastard had made it through the crash; it was nearly impossible to find good help.

I listened for a second or two, and sure enough, the disgruntled swearing of my irritable companion filtered through the wreckage.

Heaven did not like me.

Several people gathered around the entwined carriages, trying to help the driver of the other mechanical carriage and his obstreperous child, who sounded similar to a dying dolphin; the delicious smell of their enflamed my desires.

And there was only one way for me to solve this dilemma that made my fangs ache with desire - feed.

Willing the ancient power of my father's father, I dissipated my body into a cloud of mist and slowly floated out of the collage of metal, reappearing in the shadows of an alleyway. A rather large African wearing a pin-striped suit stood at the entrance of the alley, watching the "tragic" scene while fondling the arse of a female companion.

"Thank, the dark gods," I whispered, reaching forward, silent as death.

I grasped him by the back of his neck and pulled him into my darkness before his female companion realized what had happened.

Ah, that was much better.

I stepped out of the shadows of the alleyway, wiping the African's blood from my mouth, and took my place beside his former companion.

"My dear," I purred, "what could have caused such a tragedy?"

"Well," she replied, pushing strands of blond hair out of her blue eyes, "I was standing on the corner, waiting for a trick because I really needed the money for my-"

"My dear," I whispered, transfixed on her pulsating jugular vein, "the accident."

"Oh, I'm sorry," she replied, staring at my lengthening fangs. "Now... where was... oh yeah, well, I noticed this white-haired old geezer driving that limo over there." She pointed at Randal as he crawled out of the wreckage. "I tried getting his attention, but he wouldn't look at me. He just kept on whistling like he hadn't heard me and... "

God, I hated blondes.

"Well, then I flipped the old bastard off, and just about that time," she pointed to the other part of the wreckage, "another car just appeared out of nowhere and slammed into the side of the limo."

"Thank you, my dear," I replied, snapping her neck.

I hated wasting food, but I was already full.

"Hey mister, why'd you do that for?" asked a high-pitched voice behind me.

Another street urchin holding a bag of trash pointed at my victim and then gasped as I disposed of her in a rusted container holding several black bags.

Yes, this would be a bloody night.

"Hey mister," he replied, revealing a rather large knife, "I'm talking to you!"

Alas, I rarely played with my food.

After forcing the urchin to slice his throat, I walked through the crowd, parting the sea of cattle with the darkness that swirled around my heroic presence. I wanted to inspect the devastation, but the irate driver of the other mechanical carriage appeared, blocking my path.

"You know that was your driver's fault," he stated.

"Do tell," I replied, crossing my arms.

"I was just coming back from my office, enjoying a conversation with my son, Billy, when all of the sudden your car appeared out of nowhere and slammed into mine." He pointed at me. "Your driver nearly killed me and my child!"

Then he grasped my shirt, a bold move, to say the least.

After tearing the irate driver's head from his shoulders, I turned back to find Randal holding the obstreperous child, smiling a bewildered smile.

"Randal, please, not another child."

Originally published in Morpheus Tales #2, October 2008

All Pink On The Inside By Steven Lee Climer

"I am not a serial killer, Mr. Aronson. I abhor such meaningless violence by stupid middle-aged white men who have some mental defect or need for domination and punishment, or retribution. I am not your judge or your jury. My acts have a specific purpose, you see. And that is to erase illness. To help men see illness and correct it. Sadly, though, the first step is recognizing the illness and that is where my process has to begin."

The speaker kept to the shadows of the small windowless room, careful to conceal his identity. The bare room was made of concrete blocks, and the lighting was purposely dim in most spots. Mr. Aronson couldn't concentrate though. He wanted to take in as much detail as he could for the police when they found him. But he'd been beaten unconscious earlier and blood had crusted in his eyes. Pain was myriad bee stings in his mind. He was also securely tied to a chair, starving, dry with thirst, and with a thick nylon collar with a black box attached to it strangling him.

"Recognizing irrationality is a key step our society can take to better itself. Hate and racism are mental illnesses, Mr. Aronson. You will soon see what I mean. There is no biological pathology for hate or racism to exist; therefore it is an irrational mental illness that can be treated. But recognition is the first, most difficult step. Can you make that step where others couldn't? You could help humanity in untold ways."

The speaker approached Mr. Aronson from behind, still out of view, and whispered: "I've been watching you for quite a while. You, Sir, are at a pivotal point in your life right now. In fact this could be a pivotal point in humanity – if you wish it to be." The speaker snatched Mr. Aronson's blonde hair in his fist and yanked it forcefully backward. "Don't be afraid to talk to me. This is where your life – everyone's life – can change. You can even change my life in the next ten minutes. If you can read the clues and make the right choices. Again I do not judge you I have nothing but progress in mind. I love the human race, and I weep when I see people like you – people so poorly socialized, programmed, into thinking skin colour or superficial preferences affect the human soul. I'm here to help you unlearn all of that. Can you do that?"

Mr. Aronson dared to speak. "Why are you doing this to me? Who are you? Why me?"

The speaker pushed Mr. Aronson's head forward violently. "That's all? Still thinking so egocentrically? It's all about you, isn't it?" The speaker moved around the small room. He stayed in the shadows to remain unrecognizable.

"Tell me who you are?" Mr. Aronson's head swam with confusion and pain. His multiple wounds and lacerations made concentration a mountainous ascent. "I don't know what you mean... I... "

"I guess I was expecting too much of you, Mr. Aronson. I can help you there. Usually those who are ill do not know it. It takes discovery and reflection – an ability to unlearn. To put the mystery together and rise above it. Brutality has its place in the world. Brutality is not a mental illness. It is actually a fantastic journey to discovery. A wonderful learning tool. Perhaps better described as an unlearning tool. But you must forgive me, I talk too much about my passion for human beings.

"Are you familiar with shock collars for dogs? There's one around your neck." The speaker held up a dark rectangular object. "Behaviour can be modified with electricity. They can be very effective tools of unlearning."

The speaker pushed a button and a faint high-pitched tone sounded from below Mr. Aronson's ears. It was instantly followed by a vicious, painful shock to the side of his neck that made him shriek.

"You sound like a puppy, Mr. Aronson." The speaker gave him another shock. "We are now ready for our conversation, and this little device will help you tell me the truth."

"Please..." First the tone sounded and then a shock hit the collar, crumpling Mr. Aronson like paper.

"Only speak when spoken to, understood?" He circled around a chest-high box near the table. "Life is full of simple decisions. I don't need to tell you that. You've been making simple decisions all your life, right? Black or white? Yes or no? It's just that easy. Well, that's all you need to do to change the world, Mr. Aronson. If you answer correctly and prove to me you have unlearned your poisonous habits, I will give myself up to the police and let you live. If not, you will help me continue my quest to erase hate and racism through pure scientific reasoning. Have you anything to say? I won't shock you."

"I'm so confused... " Mr. Aronson's throat was raw and raspy. "Who are you? How long have I been here?"

"I figured you would still be ignorant. Let me inform you. After all that is fair and equal isn't it, to start on a level playing field? It is the American thing to do." The speaker paused. "Even though you were defeated in the state elections five years ago because of your racist and hate-filled rhetoric, it doesn't mean you have been forgotten. Your defeat was the catalyst - when I decided it was up to me to expose the truth about racism and hate. They are irrational mental illnesses that can be cured."

"You're the mentally ill one," Mr. Aronson grumbled.

The words got him a wicked shock. "Always blaming someone else for your problems – that's such typical behaviour of a racist. Blacks are to blame for crimes. Blacks are the reason your kids didn't get into law school because of affirmative action. The gay man is the reason AIDS has killed so many. The Arab man at the gas station sets gas prices just to screw you. Women have taken away good paying jobs from more qualified men." The speaker paused again, his breathing was more intense and passionate. "These are your own words, Mr. Aronson."

"Those are my beliefs," Mr. Aronson stated. "I'm not the only one."

"And that is yet more proof of my point that racism and hatred are an epidemic mental illness that can be cured."

Mr. Aronson dared to speak again. "If you're so sure, tell me how?"

"The proof is right before you," The speaker said. "Let me 'ax' you a question. What am I?"

"You're a black man," Mr. Aronson spat.

"How do you know?"

"I can hear it in your voice when you talk. You want to 'ax' me a question instead of 'ask.'"

Mr. Aronson got another sharp shock from the collar that felt like piranha teeth. "Wrong. I knew you'd say that if I 'axed' you a question. Typical stereotyped racism."

"Then what are you? Who are you? Why the games? If I'm so wrong and sick then help me."

"If you can't figure it out on your own then my point is made, Mr. Aronson." The speaker sighed, his voice lilted with excitement. "And to support my point with some primary research I will now 'ax' you another question. Think carefully because your life depends on it. Also, if you answer correctly, I will turn myself in and face any consequences the racist justice system has for me. I have high, high hopes for you, Mr. Aronson."

"What is the question?"

The speaker removed an old bed sheet that had been covering a small ancient Maytag avocado green refrigerator that Mr. Aronson just now noticed. He opened the door and brilliant light spilled as if heaven had been inside. The speaker took out four plates covered with domed stainless steel covers probably stolen from some hotel room service. He uncovered three of the four plates in quick succession. In the cool dimness of the room, Mr. Aronson could see a red, moist object that looked like an organ or tissue of some sort.

"There are three hearts here. Human hearts. Hearts I went to great lengths to procure just for you."

Mr. Aronson gagged at the sight of the dead human hearts on the white plates. "No. No, this is all wrong. Stop this."

"Only you can stop this." The speaker uncovered the fourth plate to reveal it was empty and clean. "This one is for you if you cannot solve the mystery."

"Please... I have a lot of money... I can pay you... "

A shock silenced Mr. Aronson. "Another racist attitude! You think you can just buy your way out of anything? A rich white man. Money breeds hate and racism. How many poor are black, Hispanic, or anything but white?"

The speaker continued. "I have a short story to tell you about each of these 'hearts' to help you weigh the evidence. The clues should help you decide. You may even recognize some of the stories. And let me remind you of how much trouble I went to just to get these for you.

"One of these used to belong to an acquaintance of mine. The poor man was a crack head who just got out of jail for the third time for various minor offences. He was only 25, black, no father to speak of. He had three kids by three different women on welfare - public assistance if you prefer a more benign term. His heart is here before you. But which one? I have a picture of him for you to consider."

The speaker pushed a grainy mug shot of the young man close so Mr. Aronson could see it.

"Also here is the heart of a gay man. He liked to party and had a lot of 'friends.'" The speaker produced another photo, this time it was of a handsome blonde that could easily have been an Abercrombie & Fitch model. "Too bad he liked dudes, right? Or do you like him, too? You've got a lot of skeletons in your republican closet. Is that one I missed?"

Mr. Aronson had nothing to say.

"Lastly is the heart of a handicapped woman. She was crippled by a drunk-driver who happened to be a middle-aged white guy who got a suspended sentence simply because he had connections in the courts." The speaker presented a final photo of the older Hispanic woman.

Mr. Aronson's stomach fell into his bowels. "I know her." He whispered.

"Of course you do," The speaker said. "You were the man who hit her."

"It was an accident!" Mr. Aronson shouted hoarsely.

The speaker shocked him into silence. "All that has passed. What's done is done. You need to be concerned with the lesson before you. Look carefully at the hearts and tell me which one belongs to whom. If you get it right then you will live and I will turn myself in. You can take this epiphany to the world. Show them that unlearning is possible."

Mr. Aronson scrutinized each heart on the plates. One looked a little smaller – it must be the woman's. It was so difficult because they all looked the same. Without skin, without seeing a face or hearing a voice, he couldn't tell them apart.

"I see frustration in your face, Mr. Aronson." The speaker pushed the middle plate closer. "Is this the heart of a gay man? Is this the heart of a crippled woman?" He pushed another plate closer. "Or is this the heart of a young black man addicted to crack?"

Tears streamed down Mr. Aronson's face. "I... it's... I can't see enough..."

"What do you actually need to see?" The speaker pushed the third heart closer. "They all look the same. Notice all three have veins and arteries. The muscle itself has a grain to it. I can see why you say there is no difference that you can detect. But you must. You must use your powers of hate and discrimination to figure out the puzzle. You only have a few minutes to decide."

The speaker put a cheap kitchen timer next to the hearts. It was set for five minutes and the time was rapidly ticking away on the LCD screen. Then, the speaker pulled a serrated hunting knife from a leather case strapped to his waist. It had remained hidden in the shadows until now. He tapped the stainless steel tip on the empty white plate, and hummed the theme from Jeopardy.

Seconds flowed through the timer, lowering the minutes. Mr. Aronson's own heart pounded, stiffening the muscles of his neck. Each heart was reddish pink. Just like his? Each heart had snaking veins that had been rudely severed. Just like his? The flesh had nothing to tell him. Each heart was made of identical tissue. There was no sign pointing to the black man's or the gay man's. Another mercury minute faded.

The speaker walked slowly away from the table. "Time is running out. Think of all the clues. Who is who? Could you really tell the difference next to your own heart?"

"I can't... I don't... I need more time... "

"There is no more time. You can see how racism and hate is irrational. You can't even tell the hearts apart from the very people you hate and despise." The speaker rubbed the flat side of the knife across Mr. Aronson's cheek. "Everyone bleeds red."

The final two minutes unspooled until only seconds remained. Then the timer beeped its death knell.

"What is your answer? Have you solved the mystery?"

Mr. Aronson didn't know. He couldn't think. His mind was tortured, confused, alive with maggots of fear. "The smaller one – that's the woman's. And the middle one is the fag's. And the one on the right is the black guy's."

The speaker didn't answer, instead he let silence weigh heavy in the air. He breathed hotly on Mr. Aronson's neck and pricked his ear with the knife's tip. "Education is the key, my unfortunate friend. Do you know what I'm going to tell the next person who takes this challenge?"

Mr. Aronson swallowed hard, "I've got a family, please... "

"So does the 'fag,' as you put it."

"I didn't mean that!"

"The fourth plate will contain the heart of a racist. Do you think they will be able to tell it from the others?" The speaker lined the knife's icy, sharp edge beneath Mr. Aronson's opposite ear precisely on top of his pulsing artery. "I don't think they will either."

Originally published in Morpheus Tales #2, October 2008

Produce By Gary Hewitt

Nothing. Not the merest hint of them knowing whether I'm alive or dead. Suits me fine. I like the company I keep. After all, who needs humans? Yet, I'm compelled to sit and gaze at a long dead screen animated by a flashing spectrum of unwanted characters informing me of a message.

My hand shakes. I don't want to look. I wish to remain where I am, a trouble to no one, a forgotten footprint, far, far from home. A finger; mine; travels to the words, open. My shoulders hunch, my back slumps. The chair I reside in squeaks in protest at my disposition. The monitor shows a bar incrementing one by one until the dreaded percentage reaches a century. At once, a man suited and adorned with the crest of Lavell's Exploration scowls in my direction. I find myself turning away from his badger face.

"Hello, this is a message for Mark Abrahams. I've been conducting an audit of our operations in the Revenant quadrant and it seems that we have had no contact from you in over fifteen years. Obviously, this is a major concern to us in regards to your welfare and the biological assets that were assigned to your mission. It would be in everyone's interest if you can firstly confirm your condition, secondly, inform us of the state of the creatures, and thirdly, explain your lack of communication to us. It is inexcusable of my predecessors not to have attempted to contact you, but rest assured this situation is being addressed."

Bastard.

Like I care about their assets. One half-witted assistant who managed to get himself electrocuted two days after arriving. Outbuildings made of cheapest steel; half-rotted now to stumpy old pegs holding up a ramshackle roof; the most meagre of fare to exist on almost damning me to certain death. Yet, somehow, I'm still going and I thank my little friends and best mate for that. If it were not for them I would have perished, out here, alone on some forgotten lunar outpost.

The message ends with a promise of sending someone to investigate. The cretin on screen is paused in a perpetual stare of inquisition. Let him send someone down. I'm staying. I made this home. To hell with Lavell's Explorations.

A large trumpet blast echoes behind me. I flick the screen off and throw on my hat; a red tube with a piece of half dead string dangling with no apparent purpose. It's going to be very warm today so I don't bother with a shirt. Damn thing is riddled with holes anyway. I toss on khaki shorts, long since faded to a dull green and snap on a pair of ebony sandals. The trumpet blasts again.

"It's ok Japonica, Daddy's coming."

I stumble bit by bit to the open door. Japonica's immense frame paces in impatience. She blasts again, impelling me to haste.

"All right, all right, I'm coming. Nice day isn't it?"

She lowers her back, inviting me on board.

"Yes, very nice Daddy Abrahams. What are we going to do today?"

I pat her immense head before stroking her under the chin. She enjoys me touching her there.

"The usual. We'll go round and visit the coop, see how everyone's doing. That is, unless you have any other suggestions."

My legs take residence on the small of her back. Once she knows I'm ready, she stands.

"I don't know Daddy. Couldn't we maybe go down and explore. It's dreadfully dull around here lately."

A sense of irascibility grips my mood.

"To hell with exploring. Why should we waste our time going hinny and ninny, here and there? Well? Damn exploring. Do you know those cheeky bastards had the nerve to message me today. Fifteen years without a peep and then, 'Oh, Mr Daddy, how are you today? How come you never got in touch? How are our assets?"

I'm gripping the flaps of Japonica's ears a bit too tight. She blasts her trunk again, forcing me to relent.

"Pardon me for asking."

Straight away I regret my outburst. Old Jappy, she can hold a grudge. I don't need it, especially now.

"Oh, I'm not angry at you my dear. It's those damn cash monkeys who'll be coming to visit. Maybe they won't come if I don't answer. Do you think they'll stay away?"

"Who knows Daddy? But, I reckon if we keep quiet they might just forget about us, I mean, no offence, but simians tend to make a mess of things as a rule."

I'm relieved. Japonica always talks sense.

"Shall we pay Colonel Davis a visit? It'd be good to see how things are getting along."

"A splendid idea! It's always a nice walk to the coop and the Colonel is such excellent company."

Her pace quickens. Fifteen years she's been here and Japonica's hardly changed. It's a shame they didn't get her a mate on the initial drop. They did promise but, oh well, she's happy enough.

A swift blast from her trunk awakens the chickens in the coop. They flutter and chuckle towards the gate. The appearance of my elephant's excitement attracts the attention of a stentorian cockerel with a twig hoisted under his right wing. He waves his baton in annoyance and shepherds the hens back to their egg laying duties.

"Confounded idlebugs! Get back to work."

The rooster directs himself to the middle of the crowd and none dare to linger. A few feminine protests are soon snuffed out with a few well-guided pecks. It was the best decision I ever made putting Colonel Davis in command.

"Good morning Colonel, I see everything seems to be in order."

A set of bandy yellow legs bob up and down in accord. He presses forward and his strutting stops once he has hopped onto a set of boxes taking him to the level of Japonica's right eye.

"Indeed Sah! The troops are performing most admirably. I would expect our yield to be up a good two percent on last week. I must say, the latest feed you have treated us to has worked magnificently."

I nod my approval. My experiment with grain and the genetic supplements seems to have paid off.

"Good, good. Well my good cock, I won't dally. You seem to have everything in order, which is good as we may be having visitors."

"Visitors Sah! Visitors! Well, then they'll not find a more organised chicken coop in the galaxy. I'll make this place spotless, spick and span. There'll not be a feather out of place on my watch."

I don't have time to say farewells. He is off to the pen again, clucking out orders. This is his mission, a challenge he aims to complete with total success. Satisfied, I urge Japonica to a nice stroll across the lunar landscape. If we have visitors, they'll find the best run outpost in the galaxy. Who knows, maybe they'll send some help. Yes, an extra hand on my farm would be a great help, a very big help.

I have locked the door in the interest of personal safety. My thoughts are awash to what words I will state in my report. In all my years of external audits, never have I found a case like this. Mark Abrahams is quite unique. I straighten my tie, sip from my cup, clear my throat. My finger engages the record function.

"This is Samuel Van Der Clerk, external auditor assigned to case Lavell Explorations lunar outpost twelve in the Revenant quadrant, with a preliminary findings report. My report focuses upon the competency of the outpost manager, and also the condition of the assets. The auditee is Mark Abrahams. There are no other employees, to the best of my knowledge."

I wipe away a realm of sweat. I refer back to my notes, unsure on how to proceed.

"Mark Abrahams has been on this outpost alone for almost all the fifteen years he has spent here. His assistant, Roy Clark, appears to have perished due to an electrical fault. Unfortunately, due to the time lapse I am unable to verify cause of death. Fifteen years alone on this moon appear to have had a debilitating affect on Mr Abrahams. It is my opinion he is quite insane."

I glance towards the door. It remains closed.

"Upon arrival I was greeted by a man in unkempt order. He was unshaven, almost naked except for a pair of ill fitting under shorts and sandals. It is my opinion he has not been concerned about his personal hygiene for some substantial period of time."

Never in all my life could I believe a man could look so feral or smell so bad.

"Despite the surprising attire, I proceeded to enquire about the facilities. At first, he seemed reluctant to co-operate, but once I pointed out the consequences of non-compliance he became agreeable. I also enquired about why he had not attempted to contact us about the lack of resources and possible evacuation plan. His answer was he felt it would be a waste of company resources as he felt his operation was an undeniable success despite the limitations. He saw it as a challenge for him and his team."

I sip again. I hear a mechanical noise from outside.

"I should note right now that the reasoning behind Mr Abrahams' mission was to see how various animals indigenous to planet Earth would cope on this outpost. It was deemed a worthwhile experiment. There were various animals that accompanied Mr Abrahams' and his assistant. However, I will only focus on chickens and elephants."

I shake my head. How am I supposed to explain this?

"I enquired about the state of the creatures. Mr Abrahams informed me that he had an elephant called Japonica. He also told me that he had several chickens, which were run by Colonel Davis. I thought that odd, as Abrahams informed me he was the only human on this moon. Mr Abrahams took me to his elephant, which was to be our method of conveyance to the chicken coop. His elephant in fact, turned out to be a dilapidated, system four, moon buggy. Unfortunately, he is of the belief this is an elephant and worse, he thinks it talks to him."

Space dementia. Never in all my years have I seen a worse case.

"Despite his delusional state, he managed to show me the chicken coop. Upon arrival at a wire enclosure, he pointed towards several empty bottles and began to address them. A large brown bottle he referred to as Colonel Davis and seemed delighted everything was in order. He asked Japonica for her opinion and believed she showed her approval, when in fact he merely pressed the buggy's horn."

Yeah. A near naked man, riding a moon buggy, talking to bottles. The people who tested his psychological profile should be fired.

"It is quite evident to me that Mr Abrahams is in desperate need of medical help. I would request that, upon receipt of my report, an evacuation team be sent with all due haste. I would state that Mr Abrahams could become violent. He seems to be under the delusion that world he inhabits is perfectly normal."

Well, that's done. I feel sorry for Abrahams though. He seems a likeable enough man despite the lunacy. My hand hovers over the send button when my thoughts are interrupted by a rattle on the door. With trepidation, I stumble towards it.

"Mr Abrahams?"

He looks down. In his right hand, he holds a spade, his naked legs caked in mud.

"You've let me down. You've let us all down."

"Sorry?"

"Japonica, Colonel Davis, and the chickens. How could you?"

He must have a cable feed somewhere.

"Now look, Mr Abrahams you're not well. Fifteen year alone in space can cause… "

My sentence is unfinished. With surprising speed he clatters me on the side of the temple with his spade. I fall, blood tricking from the side of my ear.

"Looks to me like you're the one not well Mr De Clerk. You just let me put things right."

I am unable to move as he places the bottom of the spade across my neck, touching my Adam's apple. My limbs refuse to stir. His eyes, manic, catch my own. His right foot, perches across the top of the treading position and begins to press down.

"Don't worry though; I've just the position for you."

"Well, I've got to say things are looking a damn sight better than they did a week ago. Japonica is much happier now my new assistant is helping out. Hell, he's even giving good old Colonel Davis a hand down at the coop, I never believed they'd hit it off so soon. Sure, he's a bit red round the edges but he'll be top of the class in a week or two."

He stands by the door, open mouthed, avid and unable to speak. Why did they send me a damn mute?

"You get yourself down to Japonica's enclosure and help her clear it out."

He's gone before I can tell him to help out with the chickens. Still, things are looking up. Things are definitely looking up.

Originally published in Morpheus Tales #3, January 2009

Alone in the Cataloochee Valley By Lee Clark Zumpe

"... the dark places of the earth are full of the habitations of cruelty... "
Psalms 74:20

Joe stared up into the night sky while the balsams bowed to an early autumn breeze. Tonight would be cooler than last night; tomorrow night would bring frost to the higher elevations. A Cherokee had warned him this would be a bad winter. He felt it now, too.

Joe watched the last few fingers of flame shilly-shally amidst the charred remnants of knotty logs. He would let the campfire wane, knowing the cinders would stay warm through the chill of the backcountry night.

Far behind him, Fort Caswell seemed a distant, fading memory. His abrupt departure ended a promising military career; but, under the circumstances, he doubted any one would fault him for it – the Great War had ended almost a year earlier, and the need for soldiers and officers had diminished. His superiors did not question his decision.

His long trek had taken him from the Carolina lowlands all the way up through Maggie Valley and across the Cataloochee Divide. The rough and rutted mountain roads crept sluggishly over the landscape, twisting and turning like a wounded copperhead writhing in agony. He found only a few marks of civilization sprinkled along the route: a wide array of trading posts, logging camps, and remote pastoral communities carved out of the bitter and implacable Appalachian backdrop. The land never seemed willing to surrender itself, and it grudged every inch it lost to ranchers and loggers.

The forests grew thickest along the perimeter of each tiny village, as if mounting resistance to force the pioneers out of the mountains and back into the foothills.

Half a world away, the war left a different countryside scarred and defaced. Armies had gutted the ancient fields and primeval forests of Europe. Fierce combat had fouled the air with mustard gas, and with the screams of the dying. Joe had not seen it for himself – but he had lost his two brothers in the trenches of France.

Sometimes Joe found it difficult to believe they were gone.

News of their deaths at the Battle of Cantigny had arrived almost simultaneously. The heartache proved too much for his mother to bear. The doctors watched impotently as the colour drained from her face, the courage from her voice, the vigour from her breath. In the end, she had shrivelled like wilting trillium, curling up into herself – her once-soft skin yellow and desiccated.

Joe carried with him a few last notes she had scribbled in her unsteady hands, observations for her only daughter and the two grandchildren she never met.

Before drifting off to sleep beside the embers of his campfire, Joe traced the path of a falling star as it sped across the twilight, dislodged from its family and sent spiralling through the void without apparent destination.

Some time long after sunset Joe awoke. Dawn seemed distant and inaccessible. The wind still stroked the treetops, and the chill on the air had grown more perceptible. Joe could hear the rushing waters of a nearby stream where he had refilled his canteens earlier that evening. Beyond that, though, he could hear other sounds – less palpable, but no less real.

The moon bathed the forest in a bluish-grey tint so that shadow concealed little more than natural hues. The mountains themselves glowed with an uncanny radiance. Joe felt a low rumble unsettle the ground beneath him, and he heard the clang of pickaxes striking stone. The mountain seemed to cringe with each blow, recoiling in pain.

Joe shivered in spite of himself.

He lay awake, wincing with each perceived blow, imagining the arch of each pick, and the coal-black fingers coiled around each hickory handle.

Then, he heard a scream.

Joe scrambled to his feet, searching the shadows for signs of life. The bulk of the Cataloochee Divide pitched itself against the twilit ceiling behind him; the Balsam Ridge lumbered grimly to the west, and Mount Sterling ascended from the boulder-strewn banks of Cataloochee Creek. The recurring collision of metal and stone intensified, and the valley floor throbbed with inexplicable misery. Joe felt the sharp tooth of each pickaxe, felt the earth tremble beneath man's instruments of torture.

In the next instant, he believed himself overtaken by madness: Joe heard another scream...and another. This time it was not a not a single, solitary scream piercing the dusk – this time, Joe heard a symphony of grief-stricken cries. The basin buzzed with disembodied shrieks and howls.

Then, silence.

Above him, the celestial sphere crept slowly toward the distant dawn. The forests huddled in their self-authored shadows, seemingly oblivious to the entire event. Joe reluctantly dismissed his apprehension as calm slowly returned to the valley. Knowing sleep would not return soon, he took up a spot on the ground close to the remnants of his campfire and prodded the cinders with a short twig.

A sooty appendage burst forth from the crimson embers, thrusting up into the air, desperately searching for something solid. Barely recognizable as a human arm beneath the charred and blistered flesh, Joe cringed as it flailed about – black fingers squirming pitifully in the moonlight. Before he could fully react, the seared hand had found him, violently clutching at his flannel shirt, tugging furiously.

Joe grunted and gasped as he struggled to his feet. He grasped the mutilated arm, pulling with all his strength. Orange sparks erupted into the air. In an instant, he had hauled someone – something – out of the remains of his campfire and onto the forest floor. There, before him, lay a thing so disfigured, so tormented, and scorched, and abused, that it had ceased to be human. Tattered skin, and jutting bone, and unhealed wounds, comprised this victim of unearthly torture.

"Please," the thing whimpered. "They'll find us if you don't hurry."

Joe knelt by the suffering man. The wretch was so close to death that Joe had nothing to fear, and he found himself offering the man water from his canteen.

"No time," the man said, "Don't you see? You've got to get him out."

"Get who out?" Joe said, fighting back waves of revulsion and nausea. "Where were you – where did you come from?"

"Below – the tunnels – they're everywhere, beneath every city... "

"Was there an accident?" Joe eyed the dying man's twisted, gruesome body – recognized the telltale signs of torture. The broken shackles on his blackened legs confirmed his intuition "Who did this to you?"

"Them... Les Habitants des Endroits Sombres – the Dwellers of the Dark Places. They've always been there, below the surface." Bloody tears cascaded down his grimy face, scabs wept and slivers of burnt flesh fell to the ground. "The Frenchmen warned us about them... they came in the night, took us from the trenches." The man lifted a hand to wipe the tears from his cheeks. "God, Joe, you've got to hurry... Josh was right behind me – get him out, Joe – get him out."

At that moment Joe trembled. He cursed himself for not seeing it earlier: This miserable thing barely clinging to life had once been his brother.

"Jonathan?" Joe slipped a hand beneath the man's head, lifting it gently from the ground. "Oh God, Johnny?"

"Joe, get in there... they'll find him – they'll find all of us."

Joe did not hesitate. First, he thrust an arm into the embers – and, finding no base, he dove in headfirst. The warmth of the coals in the fading fire stung as he passed through the portal, but the heat he faced on the other side surpassed any pain he had felt in his lifetime.

Below ground, he found himself in a cramped tunnel vaguely lit by distant, raging fires. Instantly, his flesh roasted on the bone, singed by some far-off conflagration. Joe's eyes burned and his desiccated lips blossomed with scabs. Unseen flames sent short-lived sparks of light through the passage, crafting long epochs of darkness punctuated by brief moments of illumination.

"I'm in hell," he muttered, struggling to keep his sanity.

"No," a voice answered. Joe circled around on his heels, scanning the ephemeral radiance and the pools of pitch for signs of life. For a moment, the shadows slithered aside, revealing a crouching form. "This is not hell. You'd have to be dead to be in hell."

"Josh?" Joe started to move toward the sound of his brother's voice.

"No – don't come closer. You'll lose the portal. I don't know how John found it in the first place." Josh – five years older than Jonathan and Joseph – strained to his feet. He inched out of the shadows awkwardly, grimacing with each arduous step. "You two always had a gift, though – you had a connection that went beyond blood."

"What is this place?" Joe glanced toward the ceiling of the tunnel. Only a faint, crimson ring set apart the portal from the rock.

"Another world – a world within a world." Josh shook his head. "The Underworld of mythology. Only, there are no gods down here – just men and monsters." Josh paused a moment, then murmured "Monsters and slaves."

"We have to get out," Joe said, tugging on Josh's arm. Though still cloaked in shadow, Joe could feel blisters and lesions peppering his brother's flesh. "We have to get back home – Johnny's waiting for us."

"You'll have to help me," Josh finally slumped forward onto Joe. "My leg's broken – I can't…" Joe quickly adjusted himself so he could lift Josh up into the portal. As he steadied himself, Joe heard the sound of pickaxes break the long silence. Distant screams echoed through the caves. "So many men," Josh said, gazing down the passage. "They used the cover of the war to take as many of us as possible – to carve out their tunnels, to work in their mines, to forge their weapons. To them, we're no better than beasts. Our lives mean nothing."

"What if they follow us?"

"Don't worry," Josh said, his arms stretching toward the ceiling of the narrow passageway, "I think we're safe now... I haven't seen any signs of them since we escaped."

Even as the words whispered over Josh's tumescent lips, something wormed through the gloom farther down the tunnel. Joe could hear it hissing above the hammering clatter of enslaved, wailing workers.

He thrust his brother through the portal, sending a shower of embers cascading down into the tunnel. In the sparkles of glistening orange light, Joe saw something peel itself from the shadows – something impossibly reedy and sheathed in a husk of emerald scales. Frozen in horror, air caught in his lungs, he waited anxiously for the next flicker of light from the distant raging fires to expose the face of this underworld atrocity.

Only its eyes slipped from the shade: Narrow, askew, and hideously scarlet in hue, the shimmering orbs pierced the darkness and scrutinized him – examining him from head to toe.

Joe felt his brother seize him by the collar – felt his own legs push off the floor of the tunnel. Beneath him, the serpentine beast coiled against rock. It hissed and thrashed its long, tapered tail, as its two skeletal arms clawed at the darkness. Joe flinched as he passed through the circle of cinders, shook as the frosty air of the Appalachian night bit into his flesh.

"Christ," he yelled, crawling back onto the valley floor, "What is it?"

Josh was too busy to answer him. He pried the canteen away from his brother's rigid fingers. Jonathan stared grimly at the heavens, his eyes now void of life.

The reptilian beast burst through the faintly glowing ashes of the campfire, hissing and growling. Its scrawny arms scratched the ground as it strived to pull itself out of the underground passage. Joe kicked dirt and rock in its face hoping to drive it back into the bowels of the earth, but the beast only grew angrier.

The torrent of creek water gushing from Joe's canteen cooled the embers in the fire pit, blotting out the orange and crimson specks glowing in the coals. The creature shrieked in agony, first pulling, then pushing itself into the ground. The portal solidified as the water extinguished the vestiges of the fire, and the reptile-like thing finally collapsed.

Cut in half, the beast twitched dreadfully until the first light of dawn crept into the valley. Beneath the sunlight, the thing's scaly hide sizzled and cooked.

Josh finally fell to the ground, all his energy depleted.

"Is it over?" Joe watched as the beast dissolved into a tarry heap of bones. "Will they come back?"

"No, not for us, not here... " Josh sat up, gazing at poor Jonathan.

"The war is over," Joe said. He suddenly realized how long his brothers must have suffered in servitude. He remembered the Battle of Cantigny, wondering how many of the casualties had actually been snatched by the Dwellers of the Dark Places – how many other soldiers in other battles had been lost to the underworld beings. "Some say it was the war to end all wars."

The sun hovered over the slopes of Mount Sterling, chasing shadows across the basin. The brothers would have to dig a grave for Jonathan before they could move on toward the next settlement, and it would be slow-going with Josh's leg. They would have to hike all day and well into the night, but Joe knew they would keep moving.

Neither one of them wanted to spend another night in the Cataloochee Valley.

Originally published in Morpheus Tales #3, January 2009

Execution Day By Alan Spencer

"You'd think the convicts would be used to dying," Carl Oledo laughed. "But you, Drew Grossman, are shaking in your pants. It can't be that bad if you know you won't die when it's over. Execution Day should be a day at Wrigley Park."

"That's the thing," I answered. "I don't know if I'll come back each time or not. Never do. It's not a sure thing."

The buzz of the electric shaver deafened the barber's reply.

I couldn't recall what crime I'd committed to land myself into Yearling Prison - Yearling Creek, Connecticut. It was a modest facility that harboured one hundred and fifty prisoners. Two years ago after the "Once Isn't Enough Ballot" was passed, the prison was erected. Yearling Prison was a barren chunk of land guarded by twelve-foot perimeter fences, a surrounding moat, and armed guards ready to pick off marauders at their posts. It was taxpayer funded and state-regulated. The bottom line: each death row convict had to pay for each life they'd taken, execution by execution, until his or her debt to society was repaid.

"Your head's shaved," Carl sighed, stanching sweat with a folded up dew rag from his forehead. He brushed the shavings from my shoulders with a rolled newspaper. "Off you go to fry."

The jailor, a burly man by the name of John Oaksted—and his name made sense, his hair and eyes the color of dark oak—escorted me from the leather chair with the clink of cuffs and a wooden baton shoved into the small of my back.

"Next visit is Dr. Sturgens," John recounted with a smile. "Maybe this time will be your last, Grossman. It's always fun to watch you soil your pants time and time again before the big day. People like you are always sorry on execution day."

Ward Seven, Prisoner's Chambers, Oaksted guided me past my fellow inmates. He kept jabbing the baton into my back just the like the time I jabbed the barrels of the sawed-off twelve gauge into Marge Stenson's back at the First Mercantile Bank; she suffered a stroke when I handed her the gym-bag to stuff her drawer's offerings into. The shock of the old woman falling onto all fours and foaming at the mouth urged me to pull the trigger. One shot to the chest. It was the fastest cure for a stroke.

Or was that Barry Unger's stick-up? Before I could decide, voices from the cells beckoned me. There were eyes peering through license-plate sized slits behind wrought iron doors. Fingers poked out, others able to fit their arms up to the elbow.

"Drew," Billy Ingram caterwauled. "You're not dead yet, huh? - not through with 'ol Grossman the Hartford Hatchet Killer. Beheaded your wife and gave her a bath in Silver Lake for two months. Where's the rest of the heads you took? They found the bloody knapsack in your Jeep, but no heads. What did you do with 'em, Grossman? Ten heads are better than one, ten heads are better than one! That's what my pappy used to say before he took mine!"

"You should've hid those noggins in your backyard."

"That's how he got caught."

"No, he shoved them down the garbage disposal. It caused a pipe to burst. The Hartford County's Water Control arrived at the house, and that's when they found Drew's heads."

"Or did he cut up their feet?"

"He used to be a podiatrist, remember?"

"No, no, no! Sicko ate the parts, remember? - ham-bone after ham-bone. And Drew's a Jersey boy, he isn't from Hartford."

"You're both wrong, he's the Hartford Hooker Strangler, and he ain't from New Jersey."

Hartford didn't sound familiar to me nor did New Jersey, and Silver Lake was also a smoke screen.

Chuck Passman's thick hand reached for me through his cell's peephole, the fingers dripping water. The man jammed his fist into the toilet and flushed it until he flooded his cell. It was the same fist that broke his wife's nose and crushed her larynx; she was selling herself for dime bags of heroine in Brooklyn.

"Fry me, bake me, shake me, but don't wake me!" Chuck's bulbous eyes danced. I couldn't make out his entire face, but he was smiling with the demeanor of an adolescent boy. "Today's another execution. Carve another notch into the wall. Does that make ten, Grossman? How many more times before the last execution?"

Fists and shoes rapped against the cells, church bells for an execution. I scavenged my memory for how many times I'd been executed and couldn't remember.

"They made my heart explode," another convict jeered. He was a pair of gritted teeth from a peephole. "My heart wouldn't stop pumping blood. They kept giving me transfusions, and I kept bleeding. I spurted ten gallons before they let me die."

"They tied my legs and arms to horses," Trey Adams barked, the two glints of eyes like a dog in the dark. "They whipped the thoroughbreds, and they charged away ripping every appendage from my body. Talk about a rush! Thank God they didn't tie it to my most important limb."

"- not that you'll ever use it, Adams."

Another garbled warning: "They removed my skin with sulfuric acid and rolled me in salt. They hoisted me up for those onlookers to watch me twitch and bleed. My death was like a baseball game to them. I'm sure they were cracking open peanuts and slathering ketchup on their hotdogs as they watched. It took me hours to die, and it still didn't kill me. The warden plugged a bullet in my head when the show was over, and I'm here again!"

I tried to distinguish the speaker, but Oaksted was quick on his feet. He shoved me down a different hallway corridor. Each access door was locked with a pass code device.

Oaksted grunted. "It's always a hoot to listen to 'em. They don't know who they are or why they're here, but they sure have a field day making things up." He focused on me again. "Dr. Sturgens's office," he announced. "This is what you get, murderer. Again. Sometimes even I forget what the hell you did with all their blather on the cell block."

Two other wardens, Peter Weldon and Daniel Jacobs, stayed back in the shadows of the room. Dr. Sturgens toiled at her fold-out table organizing her supplies, while I was strapped in a steel chair. Dr. Sturgens checked my blood pressure, pulse rate, eyes, ears, and nose for blockages, and kneaded her hands along my abdomen for concretions or tumors. They weighed me with the built-in scale in the chair. "His heart still beats," she sighed, listless in her work. "He'll be good to go soon."

The moment arrived for my injection. It took under an hour for it to work; the effects lasted a month - "The recuperating drug," is what the FDA called it. It had many nicknames: the anecdote, the serum, death-row juice, never-play-for-keeps, warden's humdrum, dying man's eulogy, the redeemer, hell's reprisal, and stay-of-execution. The needle poked into my forearm; Dr. Sturgens completed her task in less then five minutes. The injection had something to do with rebuilding dead tissue and blood cells or injecting a steroid boost to the body's metabolism and recovery rate. Nobody explained it to me in full detail, even when I asked.

Then the vision flashed: a woman's head jutting out from a knap-sack. Her face was ivory pale, the eyes sunken into the head, the mouth agape and missing the tongue. The head had been crudely severed from the neck, removed partly by hand. I stood above a wishing well, many of the bricks corroding around the brim. The smell of salt lingered in the air, and it was in the late evening. Woods surrounded me, the treetops rattling in the breeze as if to point me out. I dropped the sack into the well and awaited the reassuring "plop." Her name was Elizabeth, Lisa, Liza, Laura, Kim, Kammy, Katrina, Katie, Kat, or was it Mary?

Nobody said I dumped parts down a well, and I didn't believe so either. That was Carlos Hillman. He didn't believe in burying the parts; he wanted to move them at a moment's notice if needed, and wishing wells were the perfect method of storage.

"Grossman looks stumped like the rest of 'em," Dr. Sturgens said, breaking me from the morbid daydream. "The drug shuffles their thoughts and ideas around, not that they need them. It's hilarious to hear them talk on Ward Seven. Amnesiac freaks."

"It could be a placebo drug this time, Grossman," John threatened. "Who knows when your final sentence is up? - you sure don't! The injections are expensive. Did you know that, Grossman? Families like the ones you ruined shell out the big bucks for this. The "Once Isn't Enough" ballot passed without a hitch in forty-two of fifty states. I'll pay an extra quarter of a penny of sales tax to watch you squirm again. Hey, they might've found another one of your bodies in Lake Michigan; a fisherman snagged a real whopper, a real barnacle-face. Times almost up, Grossman. Let's move."

Down the hall, Priest Gary Haynes looked me over and shook his head. He kept the Bible wedged under his armpit, and he lit a cigarette. "God forgive you," he said after exhaling. "And you know the rest."

The door adjacent to Dr. Sturgens's office opened from behind me. John guided me to a conference room with three rows of chairs and a Plexiglas window looking down to a room below. Each seat was occupied by couples and families dressed for church. I counted thirty people total: eight children and the rest adults. A stern man in a corduroy jacket and pleated pants in a walker, ambled up to me. He checked me over, putting on his glasses. John stepped between us sensing the man's anguish. "It's you. You strangled my Beverly. I relish every time you die."

"You'll burn in hell!" a woman shouted, holding up a video camera. "When you finally get there."

"You murdered my daughters," another man shouted in a beige leisure suit, bobbing a sign with a picture of two young college girls. "May God never forgive you."

"The blood is still on your hands!"

"Fifty executions wouldn't be enough."

"I'll still enjoy this one all the same."

"Hell has plenty of room for the likes of you."

"God curse the womb you were born from."

"My children like watching you suffer."

The warden ushered me from the pool of incensed onlookers. The chain rattled a song that accompanied me down a set of twenty-two concrete stairs.

"It's time to find out if you're going to die, Grossman."

A steel water tank waited at the bottom of the stairs. Cameras were aimed at the brim. Reporters conducted interviews to onlookers.

"Any last words," Oaksted asked, rolling his eyes. "You have been sentenced by the state of Connecticut for the murders of... "

How many life terms, I thought. The exact number eluded me. And who did he say I killed? I didn't recognize the names.

I recalled paddling on a pontoon boat, the water's surface oil black. I heaved a tied-off garbage bag into the waters, and the shape sank with a gargle and slew of bubbles. Blood stained my hands. A pair of pink running shoes and a white windbreaker were wadded up next to a used hacksaw wedged between my feet.

But I didn't have any boating experience. It could've been Gary Ponka, but he was a speed boat aficionado. He diced the evidence in the propeller and let the fish feast on the remains.

Oakstead shoved the baton into my back tearing me from the inner debate. "You don't get last words. I've heard them before!"

I was hoisted onto a platform. The two wardens kept me in my cuffs. "Jump into the water."

"Can I ask one question—?"

Then, I was pushed. I thrashed and swam to reach the surface, but the top was slowly blocked by a plastic covering. I pounded to smash through, but it was too thick.

Cameras flashed. Hands clapped. I swallowed water. The oxygen in my lungs was released. The convulsions for air, my limbs battered the steel walls. Lights blared and brightened the waters. I couldn't hide from them. Five minutes turned into ten, ten into fifteen, fifteen into thirty, thirty into an hour. The din of the crowd didn't let up. One last detail returned to me, the same detail that arrived moment's before my death: the executions performed at Yearling Prison were never final.

Originally published in Morpheus Tales #3, January 2009

Snow like lonely ghosts... By Nick Day

Nobody can deny the existence of ghosts if they possess that thing called a memory, wherein the mind recalls voice, appearance, and even action. Everything that has come before has a potential to haunt...as long as one remembers. And if one is moved emotionally, or their actions easily swayed by memory, by history – because everything that has come before is history, or memory, thus ghosts – then the dead are busy at work in our living world. Many people are haunted for their entire lives, and remain so, until they die. Then they have no more room for secrets and become – themselves - a memory. A ghost.

In the city of Alton, you can walk snow-slick cobblestone streets and watch the Mississippi choke on ice, and if the clouds see fit to separate then a thousand dull reflections serve as a reminder that there is a sun still hovering above the earth, but warmth and sweat will have to wait, because the cold isn't done killing. Snow falls thick, like meat, and covers damn near everything but the persistence of man, his lights, and cars, and shopping malls where the older folks in town go to power walk, to distract themselves from their own advancing mortality. The cold outside is patient, aches bones, like the pain of being lonely.

It is here, in this cold, that we can find Lewis.

Lewis lives alone in a one-story house and in the wintertime he keeps the thermostat at an even sixty-five degrees, because Lewis is a heavy man who cannot deal with warmth and damp skin.

He pours himself some coffee and thinks about adding sugar.

"Mother."

Lewis always remembers his mother, Lola, when he thinks of sugar. Lola was a passionate woman, and round, very round, and very red. She was the kind of red that signalled bad cholesterol, and she was round because food rich in cholesterol tasted very good to her. She cooked meals that Lewis still remembers. He daydreams of dinnertime the way some men think of fucking.

When Lewis was much younger he made it a habit to run a lot because he did not want to end up like mom. When he ran he thought about leaving and going Someplace-Far-Away and forgetting life and snow.

Lewis turned eighteen and during that year's first snowfall he ran nine miles in one afternoon. When he came home he found Lola dead - in the kitchen. She almost finished making a chicken sandwich; a bit of mayonnaise coated her fingers. In his shock, Lewis finished the sandwich she had started. He sat at the kitchen table, cried and ate.

The official cause of death was complications of diabetes.

Which brings us back to sugar.

Lola died ten years ago and for the first five years after her death, Lewis refused to keep sugar in the house. It was a silly kind of superstition, but he always felt it was her love of sweet things that did her in. It was her addiction, like how Lewis started to drink all the time, though he put himself through AA and cleaned up pretty fast. Coffee, de-caf, became his social drink of choice. That's when sugar started making its way back into the house.

Lewis thinks coffee tastes like shit. So did alcohol, but when he got drunk enough he didn't mind so much. Coffee, however, needs sugar. Just like winter needs snow. Lewis bought a bag, but kept it in the tallest, most awkward of the kitchen cabinets.

Three of the kitchen cabinets are above the sink and are easily accessible. The fourth runs parallel to the corner of the room and above the old gas stove. That cabinet sits higher than the rest, to avoid the heat of the burners. Because the stove sticks out a good inch farther than the countertop, it makes it all the more difficult to get to. Lewis uses only one shelf in that cabinet, and on that shelf – the very top one – sits sugar.

After Lola died, sugar replaced jogging. Fat intake took the place of casual sex. Within three months Lewis was courting obesity and contemplating suicide. During the summer he tried a pill overdose, got sick, but didn't die.

While he was swallowing all those pills he started thinking about his mother's funeral, the sound of sobbing, and wanting those tears for himself, or at least something close. He fantasized about people wiping their eyes. Lewis wanted people to appreciate the moments they had with him, not because he was something significant to their lives, but because he was gone…fuck them if they wished they'd spent a little more time with him.

Lewis wanted to die but ended up barfing a lot.

His grandfather, his father's father, visited him at the hospital.

"Your father would be sick," the old bastard sneered.

"Why are you here?"

The old man leaned in close and shook his gut. "You always took after your mother."

Lewis turned away from him, blubbering. "Fuck you."

The old man grabbed Lewis by the face. "I came to tell you to clean yourself up," he shook, "to stop being such a fucking woman." He loosened his grip and went to the door of the room, but stopped just before he left. "If you're so lonely, why don't you go buy yourself a gun," he spit on the floor, "more reliable than pills anyways."

Grandfather never spoke to Lewis after that and, ironically, didn't follow his own suicidal advice. In a note, found below his swinging feet, the old man cited the inconveniences of dying in the winter. No gun for the old cuss, just some rope and a life that amounted to shit, and a disdain for cold weather. Lewis wondered what his father would have thought of that, having been a suicide himself.

Lewis thought of his father as often as he remembered his mother.

When his father died he was still very young, and Lola was still very thin, though she had more bruises. After the funeral, bruises became little more than bad family history, but Lola would still freeze at the top of any staircase and would only descend after a quick glance over the shoulder.

Lewis takes a sip of his coffee and cringes. He looks over his shoulder and glances toward that tall, awkward cabinet.

He shrugs. "Like winter needs snow," he says, and puts his cup of coffee on the counter.

Lewis is not a very tall man, slightly under six feet, and finds that he makes friends easier with people shorter than he is. He does not like being looked down on.

His stomach presses hard against the stove and his swelling fingers cannot reach the handle of the cabinet. He tries again, and a third time. His shirt has worked itself above his bellybutton.

Lewis sweats profusely.

He takes his shirt off and drapes it on the kitchen counter. The back of the shirt is soaked through, making it look like a Rorschach test. Like a butterfly, he thinks, and wipes his eyes.

His stomach pushes back into the stove and he's reaching again, but not for the cabinet handle. All he needs is the corner. If he can just get a fingernail under there, then flipping open the cabinet shouldn't be a problem. Lewis leans very hard. He bites at his lower lip and closes his eyes. In his own imposed darkness, he daydreams the cabinet coming open and the sugar is in his hands. A sigh of relief escapes him. He's not sweating. He's skinny. He and Lola share a coffee. Dad is home. All is love. He's got it.

Searing pain.

Lewis opens his eyes and sees blood running from underneath the nail of his index finger. Sweat runs from his armpits and around the curves of his fat waist. He begins to tear up and looks to the cabinet. It is open, barely. The sugar sits in shadow, hidden by the dark beyond the cabinet door.

He makes a fist and slams it into the stove. The cabinet creeps shut. He drops to the floor and sits with his back against the wall. "Fat, fat, fat..." he mumbles as he rubs his stomach. Blood still seeps from under his fingernail and leaves little smears across his skin.

There is a first-aid kit under the kitchen sink. Lewis pulls it out and pops it open, revealing the cornucopia of Band-Aids and antiseptic wipes. A roll of gauze and a pair of surgical scissors are packed into their own little container. Lewis can't imagine ever needing the gauze, and the surgical scissors make him nervous. They are more like a weapon than a pair of scissors.

Getting up off the floor takes a lot of work, but his forearms are thick. He grabs the kitchen counter and pulls himself up. He opens one of the kitchen drawers and pulls out a fork. He is leaning on the stove again.

The end of the fork slides under the cabinet door and he gives it a quick push. The cabinet opens wide, exposing the bag of sugar... which rolls back further into the cabinet.

Lewis steps back and scratches the top of his head with the fork.

"Son of a bitch."

He tosses the fork into the sink.

His shirt has dried and he puts it back on. He grabs the cup of coffee and takes a small sip, then forces himself to take a much bigger drink. He swishes the coffee back and forth in his mouth, but quickly turns on the faucet and slurps handfuls of water to rinse out the taste. He sets the cup of coffee back on the counter, laughs, and grabs the fork again.

Lewis is at the stove and on his toes, trying to hook the bag of sugar with the prongs of the fork. The strain causes him to fart and he laughs, a choked and guttural sound. The prongs of the fork catch the bag and it heaves forward. Lewis comes down on his heels and he draws his arm back. There is a sound.

A ripping sound.

A great cloud of sugar fills the air, cascades to the stove and even further, dusting the kitchen floor. Lewis stumbles back and hears the crunch-crunch of granules crushing beneath his feet, and somehow manages to knock over his cup, which bathes the countertop in caramel-coloured coffee. Sugar spills from the bag's open wound, forming sweet little dunes atop the kitchen stove.

Lewis picks up the cup and wipes the outside of it with a paper towel. He pours himself more coffee and opens one of the kitchen drawers, pulls out a spoon, and gets some sugar from the top of the stove.

It takes hours to clean up the mess. A combination of paper towels, pinching fingers, and a vacuum help get the job done. The sound of snow colliding against the windowpane keeps Lewis company.

He takes a shower and puts on some warm clothes. There is a grocery store nearby, and it seems he is out of sugar.

Lewis opens the front door and makes sure to lock the handle. Just before he walks outside, the hair on his neck stands on end. He looks over his shoulder.

No one is there.

"There is no such thing," he says.

Lewis closes the door to his childhood home, trapping within his accumulation of memories, but carrying in himself a wealth of secrets waiting patiently to be remembered.

Originally published in Morpheus Tales #3, January 2009

Being God By Jonathan J. Schlosser

Darrent sat in the shade of the young oak, eating an apple and wondering when he would have to kill Sarah. Grass stretched before him like a green blanket, shot through with clusters of wildflowers and raspberry bushes. The pond - the reason they'd stopped their cross-country trek in the middle of what used to be Michigan - sat off to his left. A soft breeze rippled the surface, splashing waves over Sarah's face as she swam.

Grinning, Darrent tucked his hands behind his head and watched. Sarah's powerful strokes propelled her naked body through the water with an ease that he envied - despite the fact she couldn't kick with her legs. Darrent had grown up in Chicago, back when Chicago was still a city full of people, not a graveyard full of corpses. He'd learned how to live life on the streets, but missed out on the rural life that Sarah had enjoyed. He could swim, of course; it was just ugly.

His grin wasn't for the fact that Sarah was naked. He'd seen her enough times that it no longer held that immediate thrill. No, his grin was because she suspected nothing, and that would make his job all the easier.

Christina sat down next to him, holding two more apples, and brushed her blonde hair out of her eyes. "Well, you look like you're enjoying yourself."

Darrent laughed. He reached over and plucked a second apple from Christina's hand. "I am. This is a beautiful world we've got. How could I be doing anything but enjoying myself?"

"You've got me there." Christina bit into the apple with a soft crunch. "Judging by the orchard behind us, and how clean that water looks, we could stay here for a long time. We'd have to build a shelter of some sort, but that wouldn't be too hard. That storm two days ago knocked down a lot of trees. Should be easy enough to build a cabin out of them."

Darrent snorted. "Listen to you. You act like building a house is no big deal."

"Is it?"

"I was a clerk, Chrissie, at Seven-Eleven. Not a construction worker." Darrent stood and twisted his arms around to stretch his back. "I say we keep moving, find some place where they've already got houses. Then we just move on in, take the place over, and don't have to do anything ourselves."

Christina frowned. "Any place like that could be contaminated, Darrent. If not with chemical weapons, then with radiation poisoning. Plus disease from the bodies. We can't take that chance."

Darrent watched as Sarah waded out of the water, limping on her right leg, sunlight glinting off her skin. She smiled up at him and began to towel dry. Darrent clicked his tongue against the roof of his mouth. "We'll go near the outskirts of a city and find some little farming town that was abandoned. The armies will have ignored it, so we don't have to worry about that, and there shouldn't be many bodies if the people cleared out."

"Which city?"

"I don't know. Somewhere south." Darrent shrugged. "I figure we could make for Atlanta, or maybe even head west toward Phoenix. If we can find a car it won't even take long to get there. Then we won't have to deal with the elements while we get things going again."

Christina laughed. "By things, you mean people."

"Of course." After the war, after the bombs and missiles and envelopes full of one powder or another, everyone thought the world would die. The last few weeks of fighting had been bleak, dark, as everyone expected that this time it had just been too much - Earth couldn't sustain itself with the damage Man had inflicted. And, in a way, that had been true. But it turned out that the Earth could keep on going just fine; it was Man who couldn't sustain himself.

Darrent had left Chicago before things got bad, when leaving became impossible. He'd seen it coming and figured he had nothing to lose. His uncle had taken him in near the Michigan state line, and they had waited it out. Waited for the armies to reduce themselves to nothing and the air to grow quiet again. It had, around Christmas of that year, just before Darrent's uncle had developed an infection from a cut on his hand. He'd spent a month growing delirious and wallowing in fever, then finally succumbed.

It hadn't taken Darrent long to fall in with Christina and Sarah; they'd come to his door, staggering down the interstate, and practically mobbed him when they'd found him alive. They'd waited out the winter playing cards and sleeping together - getting ready to repopulate the world, Darrent told them - and recently set out to see if anyone else had made it.

"So we keep going west?" Christina asked as Sarah walked up, jarring Darrent from his reverie.

Darrent nodded, smiling a greeting to Sarah. Her dark hair plastered against her skull with the weight of the water. He let his gaze drift down to her right leg, eyeing the swelling, and he decided it would have to be soon, perhaps even tonight, that he killed her. "Yeah. We'll hook south as much as we can and keep our eyes open for a car. The armies blew up a lot of them, but there are bound to be some left." He touched Sarah's shoulder. "How was the water?"

She leaned in and kissed him lightly; she always had been more affectionate than Chrissie.

"Great. You should have come."

"I hate swimming." He nodded at her shoes, sitting next to the oak. "Get ready. We've still got a few hours before nightfall, and I'd like to make as much distance as possible."

They began walking, not saying much, marching a slow but steady beat along the centre of the highway. Darrent still felt strange - somehow powerful - walking down the centreline, as if thumbing his nose at civilization's ideals and laws. All the sheets of paper left in Washington meant about as much now as the speed limit signs still posted along the road. He and Christina stopped occasionally to wait for Sarah; even with a walking stick, her pace had been slowing with every mile.

The land rose and fell slightly as they walked, but hardly enough to notice unless Darrent looked at the horizon. Trees lined the fields, leaves and grass still flourished. Flora had been wiped out near the population centres, where the fighting had been the most intense, but out here it ran on even more vibrantly, without the hazards of carbon monoxide or discarded bags of garbage. Human life had been holding nature back, but in the months since humanity had all but ceased to exist, the earth had roared back with a flourish. The sun dropped steadily, washing amber and orange over the horizon.

Sarah raised a hand and pointed. "This looks good, doesn't it?" She looked at Darrent immediately, eyes hoping for approval.

The small house at the end of her finger stared back with dark windows.

"Sure, hon. As long as old man Thompson didn't stick around to die in the back room."

Sarah's face screwed up in a grimace. "You think he may have?"

"We can't know 'til we check." The biological warfare had spread disease on an untold scale, worse even than the Black Death, and left almost no one untouched. Darrent hadn't seen another person alive - save for Chrissie and Sarah - since leaving his uncle's.

As it turned out, the house had been abandoned. It was a one-story deal with two bedrooms in the back, a kitchen in the east, and a compound living room and dining room in the west. They scouted it out thoroughly, wearing gas masks they'd lifted from dead soldiers, before declaring it safe.

Darrent did a bit of foraging and planning while Chrissie and Sarah looked for clean sheets for one of the beds. The foraging was for food; the planning was for murder.

Boxes lined the far wall of the basement, and Darrent began sorting through them, telling himself it was for Sarah's own good. And humanity's. Ever since she'd twisted her ankle stepping over a rock wall, she hadn't been able to keep up. Darrent figured it had to be broken, though Sarah did put a little weight on it. She was holding them back, when speed was what they needed more than anything.

"We'll have a chance down south," Darrent muttered to himself. "But at this rate, we won't make it before the next winter. Then we're all dead for sure."

That was what it came down to, Darrent decided as he finished looking in the boxes. There was no way Sarah could make it to Atlanta or Phoenix, and she would take him and Chrissie down with her if she didn't. They'd have no food, no heat, and they'd never make it to spring. For all his talk of finding a car, Darrent knew it was hopeless. The armies had literally demolished all of them as they moved across the country, crippling potential resistance cells. He and Chrissie could ride bikes - those littered the small towns like fallen leaves in autumn, their previous owners long-since dead. Sarah, however, couldn't even manage that.

Darrent pulled his uncle's hunting knife from his pocket, watching the dim light of the overhead bulb flicker off the blade. If he was going to have any chance to reestablish the human race, he had to get Chrissie to the south as fast as possible. He kept her and Sarah on birth control so far, despite his talk of repopulation, but that would change as soon as they didn't have to worry about walking so much. He could probably have a dozen kids if he tried hard enough, Darrent guessed. Hadn't the original settlers to the Americas had even more than that on a regular basis? He brought the knife up to his lips and kissed it. The sooner Sarah was out of the picture, the better.

The next few hours passed slowly. Sarah made dinner from canned fruit and soup she found in the kitchen. Chrissie and Darrent read through a stack of magazines. Darrent couldn't help but feel the weight of the knife against his side, tucked under his belt. It scared him a little, but excited him as well. He fought to keep the grin off his face. Society couldn't keep him from walking down the centreline of the highway, and they couldn't keep him from taking a life if he deemed it necessary. The sense of power was elating. He would miss her at times - it had been nice being able to pick between Chrissie and Sarah - but he would trade that luxury for the sheer feeling of dominance any day.

As the shadows darkened into full night, broken only by the lone gas lantern in the corner, Chrissie pushed herself out of her chair. She shot a mischievous smile at Darrent, eyes full of intent. "I think I'm going to bed. We walked a lot today, and I'm beat."

Darrent let his eyes pass over her body as he looked up. "Sounds good. I'll be in pretty soon."

As Chrissie stepped out of the room, Sarah cleared her throat. "Don't make me feel left out, Dar."

"I wouldn't dream of it." Darrent felt his heartbeat quicken as he walked across the room and sat next to her on the worn couch that adorned the west wall. He slipped an arm around her shoulders. "Is that really how you feel?"

Sarah shrugged, but smiled. "It's pretty obvious that Chrissie wants to be with you tonight."

"The joys of being the only man left in the world."

"Looks like it." Sarah laughed. She nestled in closer to him, her breath hot on his neck. "Well, how about you wait a little while before turning in? Would that be all right?"

"I think I could handle it." Darrent shifted sideways, and his stomach lurched into his throat as the knife pressed along Sarah's waist. But she didn't notice, or didn't give any sign of it. Darrent bent down and covered her mouth with his, feeling her arms slip around his neck. She was warm and soft and he had to fight back the desire to let her live. For a moment he almost slipped, almost gave in, but then he remembered that he still had Chrissie waiting in the other room, Chrissie who would help him recreate the race of Man.

His hand dropped toward the knife. He let his fingers touch her waist as he moved, and she kissed him harder. He slipped his hand away from her, to his belt, and slid the knife free.

Now that the moment was on him, Darrent froze. He had never killed anyone before, despite the hardships of the war, and he felt strangely like he had the first time he'd made out in the back of his parents' Buick. Not sure what to do, or what he wanted, but wanting it all the same. His grip on the knife tightened. He thought of Chrissie again, and plunged his hand forward.

The blade slid up under Sarah's ribs, scrapping against the bone. He could feel the serrated back edge jolting along even as Sarah screamed against his mouth. She tried to pull back, ripping her face away from his with terror pulling her eyes wide, but he held her close. He pulled the knife back out - it came with a wet sucking sound - and jammed it in again, higher. It passed between her ribs, puncturing her lung, and her scream turned ragged.

A deep voice, something that had been with him since childhood, protested in a whisper. Protested that what he was doing was wrong, terrible, condemnable. That God would turn his face away, send him, Darrent, into the dark, into the gnashing of teeth. But Darrent pushed the thought down, swallowed it. Because the world had died, hadn't it? It had died and there was no God left. None but him, at least. He'd heard, a long time ago, that God had created humans from dust, moulded them, and sent them forth to multiply. Wasn't this the same? He was just thinning the flock, making them stronger. Creating his own race, one that would truly multiply and survive, unlike its forerunners. It was his lot in life, and it would be hard. But he would do it. Because he had no other choice.

Darrent kept Sarah in his arms as blood and froth formed on her lips. She struggled, trying to hit him, to wrench from his grasp, but he locked one leg over hers and pinned her down. Chrissie didn't come out to see what had happened - Darrent thought she'd suspected this turn of events for a while now.

Sarah kept screaming, but grew weaker as blood and strength flowed from her body. Her breathing became shallow, laborious. As the lids began to lower over her eyes, Darrent leaned down and kissed her forehead. "It's for the best, babe. It's for the best."

Originally published in Morpheus Tales #3, January 2009

And If Thine Eye Offend Thee By Ken Goldman

"... Not understand none of it. Just know only Petey go squoosh in dark and then over... "

I buried Petey in the woods today.

No, I didn't do it myself. Mom helped, though I did the actual digging and most of the burying. She told me how to say the right words to God before we tossed dirt over Dad's rusty old tool box that held what was left of the remains. You're supposed to respect death, she says, so she wanted me to get it 'zactly right, and I did too, you bet. She used the word 'uh-propriate' a lot so I guess that's what my rest-in-peace speech was about. But to tell it true I don't see much that's peaceful about dying and I'm not sure I respect death the way everyone says I should. Seeing it close up I can tell you death is one ugly sucker and smells like rotten eggs someone left in the basement. 'Course, I didn't tell Mom none of that. She's always saying how I shouldn't question God's ways, that the worst kind of alone is when you lose your love for God, so I shouldn't show God I'm angry at him. I'm pretty sure Petey knows how angry I feel, though. At least what's left of him. To tell it true, I'm not so sure I wouldn't prefer having Petey around instead of God anyway.

It rained all last night so digging wasn't so easy. There was lots of mud, and that sludgy stuff gets damn heavy the further down you go, 'cause all that water, it just seeps into the earth like the ground is one big dripping sponge. I kept shovelling mud clumps until I managed a decent enough hole to put Petey's box into. Then I said what Mom told me to say. I can't remember all the exact words now, but they were fitting, all right, something about how God forgives all his children when they die, even his worst sinners. I guess I sounded properly respectful of death 'cause Mom, she was smiling even when she must've felt so sad. I can't say I feel so good about what I was thinking, but I wasn't scared if God read my mind or anything. Not if He really forgives all of us for the shitty things we think about him.

After I gave my little speech, I allowed Petey his moment when I didn't say a word. I spent that time remembering how he'd lick my face when I got home from school. It was just his way of saying he was happy to see me, but Mom always told me that wasn't very healthy because he had about a billion germs on his tongue. I didn't care because Petey was the best friend a guy could have.

Anyway, today Mom and me, we just stood there by his freshly dug grave acting fittingly courteous while staring into that gaping mud hole. Finally she nudged me and said, "That's enough, Robbie. Time's come to say 'Goodbye'." It's funny how, with all the stuff she told me to speak, my saying 'Goodbye' didn't seem to matter so much. But I said it anyway.

See, what bothers me is that God, he never plays fair. There was no need to take Petey the awful way he did, especially when he meant so much to me. Mom tried explaining that it was just his time, that God was ready to bring him home, but I can't see any sense in that since his home was here with me. I knew he was feeling sick and didn't have much life left in him anyway, but just the same I wanted him to stay here a while longer, and I don't see the harm his remaining alive would have caused. I even prayed, for all the good it did, asked God every night to let me keep my best friend a little longer even when I knew he was feeling so ill. God answered my prayer, all right. He told me, "Now Robbie, you know I can't do that 'cause, see, I want Petey too." Mom always says God, he likes to keep you in the dark about the mysteries of his ways, but I don't see the point, not unless God's the type that likes pulling the wings off flies. So I guess you can say God and me, we don't really see eye to eye about dying.

'Course, none of that matters much since God always gets his own way in matters like this. That's why Petey's out there among all them sycamores right now, and I'm here in my bed just missing him so. See, we used to share this bed every night, and Petey, he'd crawl into my arms and sleep right here snuggled by my side until morning. I'm pretty sure Mom wasn't crazy about his sleeping with me because of his germs and all, but she never said a word about it. Maybe she knew how safe Petey made me feel when the lights went out, and she decided to just let it go.

Anyway, that's what I'd like to believe Mom was thinking after Petey died. But if God sees things different while watching us, well, I don't much care. I might not understand what he's all about, but I think I have him sized up pretty good, and I don't think he's what people say he is.

See, I've been watching God a lot too.

"And if thine eye offend thee, pluck it out and cast it from thee... "

Book of Matthew, Chapter 18

Lord, forgive me these thoughts and for what I've done. I have sinned but I know that you show mercy. What's important is that it's finally over. Thank you, God, for that.

For years this has been a living nightmare, and Robbie has taken Peter's death very hard, even worse than when Ted left us. I wish I could find the tears but they're just not there. Maybe that makes me into a monster, too. Perhaps more authentic feelings will come later after all of this sinks in, but right now I can't bring myself to grieve. My thoughts are with my younger son. He's all I have, and life is for the living, isn't that so?

It was messy today for a burial, although Robbie didn't seem to mind last night's storm. The little guy was determined to perform his task the way I showed him, and I suppose I sounded fairly insistent because I felt I owed Peter at least an appropriate funeral. I pray the experience has done my son some good, and that Peter's dying served some higher purpose than his life was able to. From the start Robbie always looked after his big brother, blinded by his love to the abomination before his eyes. Perhaps that was your plan for Robbie all along, but your wisdom isn't for me to know, is it? Children, bless their hearts. They're so innocent, so trusting in a world whose wickedness is all around them.

Oh, I know Peter was not truly wicked, that he couldn't help being what he was. That didn't make it any easier. I'm sorry, but I could never bring myself to call that thing my son. Even now the word sticks inside my throat. I had my other child's safety to consider. Something born so horrible, you can't know what it's capable of and the havoc it inflicts. Lord, forgive me if I seem ungrateful, but I have always been an honest and God-fearing woman, and I know better than to doubt your love. I understand Peter was delivered from my own loins and that there should be some shred of maternal instinct I'm meant to experience, but how would that have been possible when I could hardly bear to watch that thing slither across my kitchen floor begging for some scrap from my table? How awful I must sound, a mother rejecting her own blood. But could any sensible woman consider that sopping gargoyle as family? What choice was I given? I did only what I felt was best.

The day I gave birth the doctors told me Peter could not live a week being so small and with flesh that looked as if it had been turned inside out. He had to slither just to move, and the organs inside were all wrong too. I felt certain he could not linger for more than a few days. But he fooled all of us, and just kept growing stronger and stronger, for months shrieking throughout the night while I cried myself to sleep fearing my Lord had truly abandoned me. Peter became so very powerful, and with those claws who knows what atrocity he might commit? Dr. Gracie told me he had never seen anything like it, but he did not call Peter's surviving a miracle. No sane man would.

After Ted left I moved Robbie and me to these North Jasper woods to avoid prying eyes, and I prayed every morning curious neighbours would not step off the path to steal a peek through my curtains. During these past months Peter seemed even more horrible. He must have been reaching some new maturity with those misshapen teeth growing sharper and his claws stretching out like twisted hooks. I had to keep him locked inside the basement for my own safety, at least until Robbie came home. I suppose that's what made Peter so sick towards the end. You see, there are a good deal of rats nesting in my fruit cellar, and lately they've been multiplying, so there must be more than two dozen down there. With Peter dripping all that sticky muck the way he always did, it was difficult to spot the bites unless you were looking for them, so Robbie never suspected. I just told him that Peter's condition was bound to make him ill someday, and that someday was fast approaching.

You showed me the way, Lord, without my having to do the deed by my own hand, for there is no torment worse than a child's blood on his mother's flesh. My most humble gratitude to you for giving me the strength to do what I had to!

I left enough garbage down there to make sure those cellar rats didn't lose interest. I watched them grow fatter and fatter, all the while knowing what I must do. A merciful God understands and forgives even the worst sinners, and, Lord help me, I count myself among them.

The other day those rats were so very hungry. Robbie was off at school, and our neighbours are nowhere near, so no one heard. Much better that way.

As for me, while I covered my ears I shouted my praise to you.

It helped block out the screams...

... know only Petey go squoosh in dark and then over...

... Petey in dark box not like. Used to other dark where mother puts him and hurt comes. Today was much hurt.

Wanted end. But only hurt, then more hurt. Petey scream and scream, then over. But in box dark stayed.

Parts of Petey gone. Little mad teeth chew Petey. Much teeth.

Rest of Petey not gone.

Whole everywhere is dark and alone. Bad, but is badder in box. Worse than hurt is the alone. Alone is so very much and now is baddest alone yet. No Robbie here in wet. Miss Robbie.

Mother not miss. Mother says Petey must not go in house, not go drip on floor. Mother shows mad teeth, puts Petey in dark. Then comes hurt.

This dark badder than other. This dark in box smaller colder with much wet. Petey not like small dark in wet cold box. No one find.

Tonight Petey scratch box. Not strong like once, but Petey can scratch and chew out. Petey love Robbie, scratch and chew with mad teeth, see Robbie soon.

Robbie Petey love much.

Mother not love, not no more.

So first Petey go in house.

At night Petey find Mother and go squoosh.

Originally published in Morpheus Tales #3, January 2009

Off The Hook By Michael Laimo

Fear and affliction nearly consumed Prescott Chase. He felt like a piece of chewed meat, ready to be spit out, stepped on. Trying to hide, he covered his face behind the frayed collar of his denim jacket, eyes darting from side to side in paranoid skirts. Quiet, clean-shaven, the stranger just ahead entered a seedy run-down tenement behind an unoccupied office building, a half mile west of Bloomsbury Square on Swan Place. Prescott followed, barely keeping pace, shrugging his shoulders in an effort to fend off the determined nighttime winds.

For a moment he took his attention from the back of the stranger's head and stared down at the jagged impressions of his worn sneakers in the soppy trash on the cement floor. The scrunching sounds they made tossed eerie echoes about the silent hallway, adding unease to the cold chills permeating his frail weathered body.

He peered back up, ran a trembling hand over his face and gripped his sore cheeks in restless examination of the numerous steel doors lining the dimly lit hallway. Shut, presumably bolted, their set permanence bisected the gray cinderblock walls with untrespassable accuracy. Distressed, his imagination contrived shadowed beings lurking just inches away behind each tiny peephole, deranged thoughts flitting in and out of their heads, diabolical sneers taunting him as if this place had suddenly become some polluted ward in an institution for the insane. As if he were being admitted as a sweet, freshman invalid.

The stranger's worn leather jacket crackled as he stepped deeper into the labyrinthine building, leading Prescott into a shaft drenched in darkness. Prescott's nerves flamed with anxiety. Bitter acid crawled along the walls of his intestines, sharp claws cleaving the inside of his skull, demanding pangs tearing at the nerve endings beneath his weathered skin.

Was this the onset of death? Absolutely, he thought. And it gets much worse than this too.

At the end of the unlighted hallway they arrived at a door. Prescott heard the faint metallic snap of a key slipping into a deadbolt. The lock popped and the stranger paced forward, inside.

Prescott followed.

"Have a seat on the couch," the stranger asserted.

Prescott was in a small studio flat that should have been left behind long ago for the rats and roaches. Paint chips serrated the walls like a peeling sunburn, a mouldering rug buckled under his feet like a slithering serpent. At the centre of the room a bar stool and beverage crate sat positioned in front of the hole-ridden couch. Lumps of yellow foam burst through the frayed fabric like scattered growths of fungi. The floor was a dusty graveyard for cigarette butts.

Prescott swallowed a dry lump in his throat, then did as he was told, and sat on the couch.

Minutes passed. He stared down at his trembling knees, compulsively running his thumbs across them as he waited. For a moment he considered slipping away but the stranger finally appeared holding two plastic cups filled with a clear brown liquid. He handed one to Prescott then sat on the bar stool opposite the couch.

The burly, nameless man, whom Prescott met a mere hour earlier at the underground rave on West Row, slowly reached down into the crate between them and retrieved a small mirror. He placed it flat on his lap, reflection-side up. Prescott's mouth watered with utter relief as the man plucked a vial and blade from his shirt pocket and cut out four powdery white lines of cocaine atop the mirror. He placed a three-inch plastic straw he also retrieved from his pocket alongside the drugs, and offered the concoction to Prescott. One handed, Prescott accepted it eagerly, like an unfed dog, staring at his own sunken reflection as he filled each nostril.

The stranger shifted on the stool, crossed his legs. "Well... how do you like it?"

"Pretty damn good." Prescott swilled a generous mouthful of the brown liquid from the plastic cup he held. Whiskey. He closed his eyes, embracing the pleasure of the alcohol washing the tingling powder down his throat, through his mucous membranes. "I've got enough money for a half," he confessed, finessing his nose as if trying to detach it. Good stuff.

The stranger took the mirror from Prescott and placed it on his lap. He leaned back slightly, allowing the shadows to absorb his features.

He raised both hands. Holding the razor in his life hand, he slid the edge of the razor blade across his right palm.

Blood poured forth. Prescott cringed, shuddered at the ghastly sight. The blade and jewelling blood reflected the dim light from above into tiny orange beams, ruby beads dripping onto the mirror. Using the index finger on his injured hand, the stranger swirled the powder and blood into a thick pinkish blend. He licked his finger, then brought the mirror to his face and lapped up every last globule. Once finished, he placed the bloodied blade back into his jacket pocket, the mirror to its place on the crate. As if his actions had been nothing outside of the ordinary, he lit a cigarette and blew out a plume of grey smoke.

Uh shit, Prescott thought. That's damn insane.

The stranger leaned forward, elbows on his knees, tombstone grin on his face. "Mr Prescott, are you at all aware that life is full of challenges? Millions of them languishing at our fingertips just waiting to be snatched up by ready, anticipating individuals like yourself? Did you know that?"

Prescott fidgeted, fear climbing two steps at a time. A haze fell over his thoughts, the stranger seeming to not make any sense. He managed to ask, "A-are we going to cut a deal o-or what?" as a strange, sudden dizziness filled his head. His fingers trembled as he attempted to clutch the armrest of the couch. Heart thrashing, he simply wanted to get some drugs and get out of there.

"Yes...a deal. That's why you're here, isn't it?" The stranger laughed. "Oh Mr Prescott, you just don't get it, do you? You follow me home from the club, you don't know my name or anything about me for that matter, and you just expect me to sell you some of that fine dope just because I told you I would an hour ago. Ha! There's a problem with that scenario, Prescott ol' boy. You see, it just doesn't work that way; it's not that easy." The stranger closed his eyes, hesitated, then said, "Sure Mr Prescott, we can cut a deal if you want." He leaned forward, eyes narrowed. "But on my terms."

What terms? I don't like the sound of this...

"I don't know if... " In an effort to speak, Prescott found himself with the sudden inability to string his words together. He felt light-headed, off-kilter. "W-Was dis a-aw abow?" The words wouldn't come. He moved to stand. A heaviness pressured his chest. A great wave of dizziness surged to his head, knocking him off balance. He collapsed to his knees like a sinner at the pulpit, reaching out and trying vainly to support his weight against the wooden crate. He couldn't coerce any strength from his muscles.

He slammed to the floor in a limp curl.

Lost in a dark cloud, he rolled his gaze to the looming shadow above, tried to see but could not make out much more than phantom blotches darting about. He did not know where he was, who he was. Alien voices sifted in and about from somewhere beyond the perimeter of his existence:

Time to cut a deal, Prescott...

...on my terms...

Blackness.

Prescott awoke.

He tried to move. And started to swing.

He panicked, eyes wide open but unable to see. He struggled to grasp onto something, but his hands found only cold air. He brought his fingers to his chest and found something there - something thick and cold, and rising up away from him.

A chain.

Squinting, he looked out but could not see. Am I blind? Darkness enshrouded him on all sides. No floor, no walls. Just black empty air unfurling away, enveloping him. Again, he tried to move. Pain racked him. Something harsh, stiff, digging deep into his torso. He explored further with his hands...

Rawhide...wrapped around my chest...a steel loop shape embedded into the rawhide...a hook through the loop...

Prescott was hanging.

"Hello Mr. Prescott. How was your nap?" The booming voice, familiar, burst through atop a cushion of white noise, suggesting a speaker. "You most certainly have quite a headache right now. That's from the codeine I put in your drink. Not to worry though. It'll wear off. Now listen close. It's time to cut our deal. All you have to do is find your way off the hook, and I'll supply you with a lifetime supply of cocaine. Simple enough, eh? And quite fair, I think you'll agree. Just get off the hook and find your way out, and a lifetime supply is yours.

The speaker went dead. Prescott struggled to hold himself. The harness burrowed deep into his armpits, producing a great burning pain that stiffened his entire upper body. Sucking in a mouthful of stale air, he reached his arms up, grabbed the steel chain, and pulled.

His body rose. His muscles screamed. His skin burned.

The bulky leaden hook slipped from the loop.

He was free.

Now what?

Holding the chain tightly, he pressed his face against the cold links. His muscles and bones screamed at the gravity hungry to claim his body. He stretched his right hand over his head, pulled himself up another notch. He repeated the technique with his left.

He held on for dear life, staring out into the darkness that seemed to go on infinitely. He recalled the evil horrors watching him from behind the closed hallway doors. Now they lurked in the shadows below, waiting for him to slip into their hungry grasp.

He shifted his body, allowing the harness to drift down his torso, over his legs to his feet. He hovered his right foot out over the abyss, let it fall.

He waited, heard nothing. No thud on the bottom. It vanished into the black, forever ceasing to exist.

He blew out a thin breath of air. Felt weak, ill, scared. He forced himself to look only skyward, and soon found the will to continue and press on, climbing the chain, hand over hand, his raspy breaths cutting through his thoughts like a rusty razor.

A draft from above blew across his face, chilling the sweat on his face and body.

Without warning a torrent of water came down on him, slashing his skin like a thousand icy needles. His hands slipped on the chain, his thoughts fixed on the hungry distance and the evil things writhing in a massive orgy below, mouths open in anxious anticipation for his body. The water trickled between his fingers, prying them from the chain. It flooded his eyes. He screamed in unison with his muscles, felt himself slipping, slipping...

The water stopped. The hiss of the amplifier darted through the chamber, and in the far distance a maniacal laughter sounded, evaporating into the heavens like a rising plume of steam. Prescott coughed and gagged. His body shivered. Nausea riddled his gut and he tasted bitter bile in his throat. He squeezed the chain tighter, hands cramping up so badly that he simply wanted to end the agony, even if it meant his death below.

Then, a hint of light from above.

Like the sun tweaking through the clouds after a torrential storm, a faint glow appeared. Using every last bit of strength, he found the will to continue, pained hand over hand, sore eyes affixed to the light as he grew closer and closer. His heart and head pounded, blood raced, nerves tearing at his skin. He barely had a breath left in his body when he realized his asylum.

An elevator access just beyond his reach, the doors wide open.

I'm in a damned elevator shaft.

He climbed to eye level, and then further, so that the landing met him at waist level. He could see an abandoned office, clouded morning sunlight filtering through filth-encrusted windows. Broken desks and chairs littering the landing, large stacks of papers left behind to await their fate with an incinerator.

Fidgeting, he slowly brought the chain to a swinging momentum, more and more, little by little, until he managed to catch hold of the carpeted floor with one trembling foot.

Blood pulsing, fighting all elements of panic, he threw himself at the landing.

A lifetime of fear besieged him as his foot slipped back into the shaft. The surrounding darkness and grey light winked away and spun around him in a disarray of monotone, forming new worldly shapes that moulded around his body in swirling spirals. As a last instinctual effort, he thrust his arms into the merging backdrop, and somehow, dear Lord, found the edge of the landing.

He hung there for what seemed an eternity, fingernails digging into the worn carpet, coarse breaths echoing towards freedom. As terror and pain twisted every inch of stamina in his body, he miraculously unearthed a previously untapped inner strength, a last reserve utilized only in instances of life and death, and pulled himself up onto the landing.

He crawled clear of the shaft, collapsed next to a chair, exhausted, pained, sucking air through his mouth in desperate wheezes.

Suddenly, a shadow looming over him.

Prescott looked up. Saw the baseball bat in the stranger's hand.

He couldn't even cringe as the stranger clubbed him on the head.

###

Prescott awoke on concrete. The sounds of traffic formed. His eyes fluttered open. Bright. Sun. People, dark silhouettes encircling him.

"He's awake," someone said. He shivered, cold, hugged himself to keep warm.

Something felt strange about his body, uncomfortable.

He peered down, saw something sticking out from his chest.

Two people helped him sit up. He looked. Badges. Policemen.

They cuffed his hands, wrenched him to his feet. He looked at one of the cops. From the 13th precinct.

"Come with me," the cop demanded, shaking his head. His face came into view, a look of disgust painted on it. "Sergeant Prescott."

Sergeant Prescott of the 13th precinct blinked. His eyesight cleared and he looked down at his body again.

Oh my God... he managed to stutter.

Taped around his naked torso were five one pound bags of cocaine.

His lifetime supply.

###

Sergeant Prescott sat in a cell, waited.

After what seemed an eternity, someone came, a guard. "Your court appointed attorney will see you now. Follow me."

He followed the guard through a hallway of cells occupied by sneering felons. Many of his co-workers stopped and stared as he was escorted through. They reached the end of the hall and entered a room with a small table at the centre. The lawyer, dressed in a suit, faced out a barred window.

Sergeant Prescott sat at the table. His escort left, leaving him alone with the lawyer.

After an uncomfortable silence, the lawyer finally spoke. "Sergeant Prescott. It's my turn for a challenge... "

Prescott cringed at the familiarity of the voice.

The stranger turned to face him. "To get you off the hook."

Originally published in Morpheus Tales #4, April 2009

Vampires Suck By Lyn Cannaday

"I want to find the nearest vampire and rip it to slimy, bloody shreds," Polléo complained. He snuffed at the air, his nose held high and his white-tipped ears twitching at Venia. She thought he'd gotten over that stupid book. Obviously not. "Vampires suck," he snarled.

"Yep," she agreed, wisely not pointing out the pun. She was an idiot; she never should have lent him that novel.

"I vant to suck your blood," he intoned in a very bad imitation of a Transylvanian accent. "I mean, have you ever heard a vampire talk like that?"

"Not really," she admitted. The ground vibrated with his low growl. "It's like there was some trial for coolness, and we got convicted without ever knowing we were supposed to defend ourselves. Convicted and sentenced to uncoolness." The line of thick fur along his spine rippled in annoyance.

"You're far more attractive than any vampire I've ever met," she promised him truthfully. She was lucky to have such a strong mate, even if this current vampire obsession was a little annoying. A breeze rustled the branches overhead, and he put his nose to the moonlit sky, scenting the wind. She perked her own ears forward in anticipation.

"Humans give vampires all the awesome powers: mesmerizing eyes, sexy accents, angsting drama, and now they get to be sparkly," he complained with a huff. "Why don't humans give us some of those cool powers? I'd love to see a movie where the werewolves weren't just bad actors in fur suits. I want a werewolf movie with a sexy she-wolf with hypnotic, silver eyes and retractable claws and the strength to tear down mountains." His eyes grew unfocused and lusty.

Leaning over, she nipped his shoulder.

"Ow," he growled.

"Serves you right for not liking my claws." She let her hand rest on his arm. Her fingers were shorter than a human's, and thick, milky-white claws curved down to a sharp point.

He shook his head at her, his ears coming forward as he leaned in and rubbed the side of his face against her shoulder. "I love your claws. I love other parts of you even more."

"Then why are you getting-" She froze when he jerked away, all attention focused on a spot north of them. Crouched in the carpet of pine needles, she scented the air that drifted sluggishly toward them. Humans.

His eyes searched the dark. Tufted ears swept forward and back, and Venia tucked her own ears close to her head, waiting for the signal.

When humans described beauty, they never understood the grace of the werewolf. Polléo's face was strong and beautiful, with piercing, dark eyes and long teeth. Preparing to pounce, his back arched and the line of thick fur along his spine rippled and shone in the dull moonlight that filtered through the trees. Muscles corded under his skin. In his human form, he was handsome. As a werewolf, Polléo was stunning.

A foot crushed a pinecone with a loud snap, and she slowly and silently inhaled, the scent of earth and pine and human sweat tickling her nose. Polléo twitched his tail once, and then launched himself forward. She leaped at the second human. While Polléo's human fell silently, hers gave a desperate shriek before Venia sank teeth deep into a pale, soft neck. Warm blood sprayed against her chilled skin.

She shredded the dead woman's shirt and buried her muzzle in the tender meat of the stomach. Polléo was already ripping liver out of his prey. The organ made a popping sound like gum as he tore it free of the viscera. He tossed a red chunk up into the air playfully before catching it.

"Seriously, why do vampires get all the good press?" he demanded.

"Humans are just strange," she mumbled around her food, too hungry to stop eating and have a proper conversation. "I don't think they like predators. They always cheer for Bambi."

"Vampires are predators. Humans like them. Hell, vampires not only kill but then they let all the good parts rot." He pulled another chunk of liver out and swallowed it whole. "If humans didn't taste so good, I'd say the planet would be better off without them."

Ignoring the odd obsession both humans and Polléo had for vampires, she ripped into the liver on her own prey.

The thump of something burying itself in the trunk of a pine tree did not disturb her, probably because the prey filled her senses. But Polléo howled his outrage and slammed into her, knocking her away from her meal. Venia reached over and bit her mate. Obsessions with vampires she could forgive, but that was her meal he had interrupted.

"Hunters," Polléo snarled in her ear before her brain could register the bright 'pop' of the gunfire. Burning gunpowder cut through the rich scent of blood, and Venia scrambled to her feet. Polléo's tail was already vanishing behind a small stand of sapling pines, and her claws cut into the earth as she raced after him.

"Shit. Aim lower," a human voice called, all secrecy abandoned now. Footsteps crashed clumsily through the underbrush, and Venia crouched low and ran harder... ran until her legs burned and her breath came in heavy gulps.

She smelled her own blood right before she felt the fiery sting of the gunshot wound. The pain forced her to run on three legs, one of her back legs tucked up close to her body, but she would not stop. Hunters were nothing more than humans - prey. She was not so weak as to fall to prey. Her lip raised in a derisive snarl at the thought.

When a bullet ripped into the tree beside her, she ducked left to avoid a spray of splinters. The ground sloped, and she lost her footing. Tumbling down the hill, she curled up tightly, trying to protect her stomach and injured leg.

"Got one!" a hunter yelled.

Venia trembled with adrenaline and rage at the bottom of the steep slope. Broken and bent plants betrayed her position to anyone with the brains to look... even a human. Then Polléo was there, his strong legs straddling her while he nuzzled her side.

"I'm okay," she whispered even though she wasn't. Her side hurt, and her good leg was burning with fatigue from carrying all her weight. As a werewolf, she healed fast, so the wound had stopped bleeding. However, she couldn't heal fast enough to keep running.

"Get to a tree," Polléo said, pushing her with his head.

"What? No." She snarled at the idea that she would leave him, but he just kept shoving at her.

"Go."

"We fight together."

"No. We don't." He rested his paw on her stomach, his sharp claws making five tiny dents invisible under her short fur, but she could feel each pinprick against her skin. "This time, we don't fight together. Now get to a tree." He snarled the words.

Awkward human feet stumbled down the hill, bringing random curses and the smell of gunpowder.

"Polléo," she whispered desperately.

He snarled at her again, showing off his teeth. The first time he had visited her pack, he had done that, and she had wanted him. Now he turned, his body whipping around so he could dash up the steep slope.

Putting her hand over the spot he had just touched, Venia willed herself back to human form, her skin itching as the fur vanished. Limping to a pine with low branches, she painfully climbed, hiding behind the thickest clumps of needles, and keeping the trunk of the tree between her and the humans.

"I know I winged one," a human called out. Idiot. He had just identified his location to Polléo, and Venia had faith that her mate would rip his throat out. She caught a glimpse of silver fur in the bushes right before a shot cracked from the top of the slope. Polléo yelped in pain, and Venia stuffed her human fingers in her mouth to keep from crying out.

"Got it!"

"Shit. It's moving."

"Downhill! Downhill!"

Two more shots fired, and Venia hugged the branch she crouched on, too numb to even cry.

Men wearing black separated from the shadows. One was fat. The other pushed through the bushes and reached in. He backed out dragging the body of her mate - her lover. She pressed her hand against her stomach and fought the urge to throw herself on them and feast on their entrails. Instead, she opened her mouth and scented the air, imprinting on her memory the smell of Polléo's murderers.

One whistled admiringly. "Damn. Big fellow." The fat man congratulated his partner with a slap on the back.

"Nice pelt!" his friend agreed. Venia knew what would come next. She pressed her forehead to the rough pine bark and closed her eyes while they skinned the thick fur of Polléo spine. The scent of his blood stained the air.

"You know," the fat one started, the stink of sulphur and cigarette rising through the still air, "other people can go for vampires. Personally, I hate those slimy, ugly bastards. Give me a werewolf any day of the week."

"No joke. Sometimes I wonder what the hell is wrong with vampire hunters. They sure never get a beautiful pelt like this one off a vampire."

"People are just crazy," The fat one agreed amiably. The sound of ripping flesh followed, and Venia wept silently, waiting for them to take their bloody trophy and leave her to grieve and howl her pain into the night.

"One day we'll find them, my pups. We'll feast on their livers." She whispered the promise as she pressed her hand over her bulging stomach.

Vampires might not sparkle or have eyes that could enthral humans, but werewolf claws were so very real.

Originally published in Morpheus Tales #4, April 2009

Under The Placenta Tree By Mark Zirbel

That goddamned tree was coming down.

Hank had had enough of it mocking him from the edge of the lot line, its trunk arched back like a cackling lunatic. The tree was really nothing but a bare pole, save for a mess of limbs at the top - that wild, barbed-wire tangle. An October wind prompted the leafless branches to chitter against one another.

"Go ahead," Hank said, "laugh while you still can!" He surveyed the top of his workbench. An orange extension cord snaked its way around slopped-up paint cans, a pile of wood chips, and a rusty bicycle tire, finally leading to the object of Hank's search: his trusty hatchet. That bastard outside didn't deserve the quick, easy death that a chainsaw would provide. No, this was going to be a brutal kill, and Hank planned to savour every vicious swing of the axe.

He stormed out of the tool shed, out into the night, and glared across the yard at his enemy. A full moon directly overhead gave an aura of operatic intensity to the showdown. How long had the thing been tormenting him? Months? Years? Hank was a little foggy on some of those details, but one thing was perfectly clear: that tree had to go.

He began walking across the lawn - slowly at first, but then faster, faster - rearing his axe back along the way. When he finally reached the tree, he thrust the axe forward with a powerful combination of adrenaline and momentum.

The blade barely dented the tree's thick armadillo hide.

And so Hank swung again. And again and again and again and again. When he finally paused to catch his breath, black syrup oozed from the small hole he had smashed into the bark.

What the hell?

Hank poked at the glistening liquid, then touched a finger to his lips. He suddenly realized that the substance only appeared to be black because he was viewing it in the moonlight; the bitter, copper taste in his mouth clearly revealed that it was blood.

Hank barely had time for his revulsion to register when a stream of blood exploded from the hole like a water main break, knocking him to the ground with fire hose intensity. The barrage stopped a few seconds later, but not before he was drenched in crimson. And lying there on the grass, soaked from head to toe, Hank had a surprising moment of clarity. Even with reality unravelling all around him, he was able to grasp onto one fact that he knew was true:

Jenny had buried Jacob's placenta under this tree.

Hank had nothing to do with it - he found the whole notion incredibly creepy. But Jenny had read that the nutrients from the placenta would break down in the soil, and the tree would absorb them into its roots. She wanted to watch Jacob and the tree grow together, both having benefited from her nourishment.

And it worked. The tree had grown healthy and strong, from nothing but a sapling. It now stood a good ten feet tall. How had it grown so much in so little time? Then again, how much time had truly passed? That's where things started to get hazy all over again. Hank's memories were like a bunch of self-contained short stories; they didn't connect one to the other like chapters in a book. Therefore, the chronology of events was difficult to gauge. Take that dinner party with Stan and Margaret Anderson - how long ago was that? Hank tried hard to recall the details of that bizarre evening...

"This lasagne is absolutely wonderful," Margaret said. "You'll have to give us the recipe!"

Jenny laughed. "Well, I'll give you the recipe, but you won't be able to duplicate it. The meat is from Jacob's placenta!"

Hank looked up silently from his plate, unable to believe that Jenny had made such a sick joke. But the Andersons just continued right along.

"And you're sharing it with us?" Margaret asked. "Jenny, that's so thoughtful."

"After our Suzie was born, Margaret whipped up some placenta fajitas that were to die for," Stan said. "I keep telling her we should have another kid just so she can make them again!"

There was a hearty group chuckle, like a TV sitcom laugh track.

Hank slammed his fork down. "Dammit... enough! Jenny was just kidding. Jacob's placenta is buried out in the yard."

"But Hank... I dug it up."

Hank knew from his wife's deadpan expression that she was totally serious. "Jesus, Jenny! How... how could you?"

"Oh, it wasn't so bad. I just had to pick out a few maggots."

"Uh, Jenny," Stan piped in, "I think you missed some." He opened wide, revealing a mouthful of wriggling, white chaos.

Hank remembered bolting from the table, but he couldn't remember whether he had made it to the bathroom before vomiting. That's where the memory ended - nothing followed but white noise and static, like a television station that had signed off for the evening.

No, wait... that couldn't have really happened, Hank told himself. That's too fucking weird, right? Then again, was it any weirder than having a tree puke its bloody phlegm all over you? Hank stared at the gangly villain hovering over him. "Okay, asshole, I'll give you this round. I'm gonna go in and get cleaned up, and when I come back, I'm bringing the heavy artillery."

Hank walked into the dark, empty house, absently wondering where Jenny and Jacob were. It didn't seem like they were around much anymore. When was the last time he had seen them? Sometimes it seemed like they only existed in his memories. Christ, so many crazy, fractured memories. Like that night when Jacob was a newborn...

Cries had echoed throughout the house, followed by a nudge from Jenny's side of the bed and a groggy "It's your turn to get Jacob."

Hank lumbered into the talcum-scented darkness, lifting the wailing infant out of his crib. He held Jacob and patted the back of his head, but with each pat came a wet, squishy sound. Hank stared at his bloodied hand in horror, then held Jacob out at arm's length, frantically searching for an injury. But it wasn't Jacob. Hank was holding a writhing placenta, wrapped up in Jacob's little yellow blankey. Its undulating membranes were the source of the high-pitched crying.

Hank threw the hideous mockery of life to the ground and ran out of the room... ran out of the house...

But where had he run to? He couldn't recall. It was yet another dead-end in his brain.

Hank headed downstairs to strip out of his soiled clothes. The basement was a cold, dark, cobwebby, storage space - mainly filled with Jacob's stuff. Hank undressed surrounded by piles of

Jacob's playthings: a toy chest, a wooden rocking horse, stacks of board games, a ten-speed bicycle...

Wait a minute! A ten-speed? Jake's not old enough for that... is he? He's only...only...

But Hank was grasping for information that simply wasn't there. Jacob could be five or twenty-five for all he knew. And yet somehow, he could remember Jacob's birth like it was yesterday.

That horrible, horrible night.

Of course, it wasn't supposed to be that way. It was supposed to be the most wonderful, joyous moment of his life. Hank had read all the books, listened to the birthing class pep talks, and heard the transcendental experiences of friends and relatives. But the moment he stepped into the delivery room, all of that disappeared. He was bombarded by screams and sweat and supernova lighting; cold, glinting steel and the stench of disinfectant; latex hands manipulating unrecognizable instruments into Jenny's gaping hole. He was too repulsed to coach Jenny, talk to her, or even hold her hand - he just sat there in a kind of trance. And when Jacob's head began to appear - all craggy and slimy looking - Hank lost it entirely. He darted from the room in a dizzy-nauseous frenzy, and found himself staring at his dinner on the bottom of a toilet bowl.

"Shame on you, sir," said a woman's voice from somewhere behind him. Probably a nurse. "Your wife needs you now more than ever! Pull yourself together and get back in there, or you'll regret it the rest of your life - maybe even longer!"

Hank puked three more times before finally staggering to his feet, wiping off his face with wads of crumbly-wet toilet paper, and returning to the delivery room. "Push, Jenny. I think one more push will do it," the doctor was saying.

Shit... isn't it over yet?

It was: the nurses were already washing Jacob off. Hank stepped around the table just as Jenny expelled a pound of red-grey afterbirth. "Christ... disgusting," Hank muttered.

The look in Jenny's eyes was beyond hurtful - it was damning. A heavyset woman shook her head sadly at Hank, and he knew immediately that it was the nurse who had spoken to him in the washroom. She fiddled with a rune symbol that hung from her neck: You'll regret it the rest of your life - maybe even longer.

And if Hank truly was damned, what sort of Hell would await him? What's the punishment for a man who abandons his wife in her time of need, who fails to see the beauty in his own son's birth? Perhaps when a man like that dies, his wife scatters his ashes under a big oak tree in the back yard, leaving those ashes to sink into the same earth that holds his son's nutrients. Maybe she recites a spell that an old nurse once taught her, a spell to bind her husband with those nutrients, so he'll be tormented by that "disgusting" placenta forever.

It's like I'm living in some kind of nightmare, Hank thought as he slipped on a clean pair of coveralls. When will it end? When the fuck will this madness end?

The wind that rattled the cellar windows didn't provide any answers. So Hank took a deep breath and marched upstairs, chainsaw in hand, ready to resume his eternal battle with that goddamned tree.

Originally published in Morpheus Tales #4, April 2009

Bloody Kisses: Blood Rose By Christian McPhate

Portraits of angels slaying demons and the Virgin cradling her son stared down upon my darkened soul, but I ignored the paintings' painful expressions and closed my eyes. The sounds of the cathedral's bells reverberated off the cracked-rock walls of the Roman Catholic Church. Electrical light from the metal torches flickered throughout the assembly hall, confining most of the shadows to the cobwebbed corners. Small tendrils of darkness, however, escaped the false radiance and infiltrated the wooden pews, where my victims prayed strange words to a seemingly forgotten god.

"Ah, to be one with the darkness," I whispered, hovering within the shadows.

An ocean of blood filled my mind with visions of ghostly-clad victims floating through my troubled thoughts, drowned goddesses in the sea of my hunger. I closed my eyes and remembered their beauty, their love, their blood that still pumped through these hardened veins.

A sharp tap on my shoulder interrupted my euphoric thoughts.

"Excuse me," a nun quipped.

"Yes," I hissed, irritated by her presence.

"Sir," she said, "Father O'Hara does not allow people to hide in the shadows." She tapped her foot in frustration, while her pulsating jugular vein throbbed with each beat of her heart.

"My dear, I am just waiting for a friend," I replied, placing my arm over her shoulder.

"Sir, the rules state that all patrons must-"

I pulled her close and inhaled the sweet aroma of blood. Her scent permeated through the shadows, driving my mind into a state of hunger.

"My dear," I purred, moving closer to the luscious folds of her neck, "you are correct; we must always follow the rules."

"Father O'Hara," she gasped, trying unsuccessfully to break free from my grasp, "doesn't like it when the rules are not-"

I lowered my head, tasted her flesh, and gagged, for it was as I feared - she tasted of salt and of bath soap.

"Sir, you shouldn't do that I need... need to- "

She was under my spell, falling into my darkness.

But she was so full of life that it took me a little longer than normal to empty her.

After several orgasmic moments of feeding, I raised my head from her torn veins, licked her blood from my lips, and dropped her to my feet, satisfied for another hour... maybe two.

Normally, I tried to avoid places of worship, but the darkness of this cathedral, as well as the nun who lay dead at my feet, seemed to bring solace to my body, mind, and spirit.

Alas, I am not perfect, and I did try my best to behave - for Randal's sake - but I was bored, and the cattle were the only creatures that offered excitement in this dreary house of the Lord.

I scoured the pews, searching for my assistant's mop of white hair among the crowd milling in front of the altar. I wanted to leave and delve into the depths of this American kingdom. I was growing tired of these god-forsaken temples that Randal forced me to visit; the taste of imbeciles made me sick to my stomach.

"Ah, there you are," I whispered, finding my crazed companion falling into the throes of worship.

Embracing the darkness, I travelled through the world of never-ending night and appeared from the shadows next to my possessed companion. Several of my prey in the row behind him fell back in shock at my sudden appearance. As they rushed toward the doors, I whispered an ancient spell of my father's father and convinced them to stay for the slaughter.

"Randal," I hissed, turning away from the frozen peasants, "it is time to leave this abominable place, for the night is passing, and we still have to find food for the obstreperous child."

Tears fell from his tired eyes – he was in one of his moods again – and I patiently waited, tapping my foot, but I was becoming agitated and famished. Then he made his way toward the confessional chambers, blatantly ignoring my request.

"For the love of the gods!"

Tendrils of shadow stretched across the cracked-stone floor of the cathedral and enveloped my body, masking my presence from my preys' eyes. I followed my companion through the shadows of the confessional chamber.

"Randal," I whispered, "you must come and watch-"

Then a ghost from my past appeared.

" -Mina?" I questioned.

For in the centre of the cathedral, where the shadows hung like a fog over the congregation, a young woman resembling my former lover sat near the altar with tears in her sparkling ebony eyes. The sight of my mistress in the dark mesmerized me, and I reappeared from the shadows and stared at her as she whispered prayers to the image of her saviour.

Then she rose and made her way toward the wooden doors that led out of this abominable place, and my undead heart beat faster. I wanted to embrace her, but two rather large peasants wearing strange-looking uniforms approached.

"Hold on just a minute," rumbled one of the uniformed men, grabbing my arm.

"Never touch me," I hissed, grabbing him by the throat, and then I broke his neck before he could mumble a pathetic reply.

"Sonofabitch," cried his companion, reaching for his weapon, but I ripped his head off before he unsheathed the metallic-instrument of death.

Blood sprayed from his torn neck with each beat of his succulent heart, covering the marbled statues of the saints.

"Such a waste," I whispered.

I rushed through the doors of the cathedral, swiftly passing my victims' corpses, and stepped into the moonlight, but it was too late – she was gone, my succulent mistress in the dark.

Alas, in my haste to reach my former lover, I had forgotten about the rest of my prey. And they found the bodies of their authorities lying in a pool of blood, and screams of the numbers "9-1-1" reverberated from the cathedral.

As I finished tearing the throat from the last member of the congregation, images of my former lover flashed before my eyes. She tormented my soul with her sparkling ebony orbs that reflected my mother's light through the depths of my mind. She was a creature after my own heart, with a desire for feeding that surpassed my former lovers.

"God, I miss the homeland," I whispered, dropping my latest victim to the blood-soaked floor.

Randal appeared next to me, smiling his idiotic smile.

Oh, how I hated him.

Then I broke the neck of Randal's priest as he peeked through the door of the confessional booth to see if it were safe - it was not.

"Maybe, I should acquire a dog... a beast of darkness... yes... yes... that is marvellous," I whispered, revealing my lengthened canines.

My annoying companion adjusted the lens of his camera, preparing to record another leg of our journey, and then his world went dark.

Originally published in Morpheus Tales #4, April 2009

Soap Sally By Randy Young

My aunt always welcomed me when I would go to her house for a visit and she would always be in the kitchen peeling potatoes, stirring something on the stove, and listening to her favourite radio show. I would take the first few minutes and lean up against the kitchen sink and listen to her as she gave me her "do's and don'ts" of being at her house, again.

"Stay out of your Uncle Mike's bedroom," she announced. "You know how upset he gets, when he knows that someone has been in there."

"I know. I have been here before, Aunt Mae," I interjected and rolled my eyes.

"If you go out on the back porch, be careful around those churns. I'm making sour kraut, and it still has a week to go before it will be ready to put into jars," she added. "You can go in the living room and work on the puzzle that I started on the coffee table, but be careful that you do not lose any of the pieces. The last puzzle that I had had a piece missing, and that big store down the road never replaced it."

I nodded and took that as an indication that she was ready for me to go on and let her finish cooking supper. She reached and turned up the radio, and stirred something on the stove and rinsed the peeled potatoes in the sink.

Aunt Mae always kept a puzzle on the coffee table in the living room, right in front of the couch. A person could sit at the couch, look for pieces to the puzzle, talk to Aunt Mae, and be close enough to answer the phone, if someone were to call.

As far as I can remember, no one ever called, but Aunt Mae listened to the same radio show every day. She was convinced that the host would call her one day, when he did his famous "drawing of a number" out of the box that you could hear him shake over the radio. No matter how many times I visited, she always gave me the same instructions about answering the phone.

"If the phone rings and you answer it, you have to say the name of the host on the radio show," she stated emphatically. "That is the most important rule to remember in winning the contest and getting the *big prize*. If you just say "hello," he will not give you the prize and then he will announce your name and everywhere you go people will know that you made a fool of yourself."

"I know, Aunt Mae." I said. "I have been here when the phone has rung before. Remember that time you almost jumped over the table and answered the phone, only to find out that it was the plumber you had called the day before about something being stuck in your sink pipe?" I grinned.

"Be careful pointing fingers at someone," she announced. "When you point a finger at someone, you have three fingers pointing back at yourself. You start doing that and Soap Sally just might come down out of those woods behind the house and cut off a finger and make soap out of it."

Soap Sally had been a feared name in our family for many generations. Anyone who grew up in our area knew about the legendary Soap Sally, who lived back in the woods in an old house with a pack of wild dogs. Her claim to fame included the stories of how she would take bad little children and make them into soap. My aunt had added that she would also cut off a person's fingers and use them to make soap.

I did not like to be reminded of Soap Sally because it made me have a sick feeling in my stomach, and then, I did not want to eat or sleep. She scared me to death, and I was sure that I had seen her walk around the corner of our house, when I was a young child, with a knife in her right hand.

Aunt Mae continued to work in the kitchen over her many pots and pans, stirring, chopping, tasting, all while setting the table at the same time. I really don't think that anyone could cook better than my aunt. She had what some people called "the gift," and no one ever went against her at the county fair. They would always lose.

"Do you really think that Soap Sally is still alive and living in the woods?" I asked Aunt Mae. "She should be well over a hundred, if she has been around as long as people say."

Aunt Mae stopped what she was doing and wiped her damp hands on the front of her hand-made apron, and stepped inside the living room door, and she leaned against the corner of the door and moved from side to side, scratching her back.

"Don't you be saying anything like that around your Uncle Mike," she exclaimed. "He will want to thump you up the side of your head so that you get a good look at his hand and see the missing finger. You won't catch him pointing a finger at anyone or talking about someone and making accusations."

She continued to mumble something, and turned back into the kitchen to finish putting the food on the table so that we could eat. I picked up another piece of the puzzle, and turned it left and then right as I tried to force it to fit into an empty place on the puzzle. It did not fit, so I tossed it onto the table and picked up another piece.

"Go in the bathroom and wash your hands while I pour us a glass of sweet tea," she called from the kitchen. "Look under the sink and get a new bar of soap. I used the last one this morning when I was cleaning out from under my nails after digging up some of those new potatoes in the back yard."

I got up from the couch and walked through the kitchen on my way to the bathroom. Aunt Mae was right about the soap, so I pulled the knob on the cabinet under the sink and the crooked door swung open. I reached into the old "soap box" and pulled out a hand made bar of soap. It had a purple flower embedded inches below the surface and smelled strong and fresh.

Rising from the floor, I tapped the door with my knee and it closed with a dull thud. I turned on the water in the sink and let it run a few minutes until the rusty water became clear, wet my hands, soaped them, rinsed them, and grabbed the towel next to the sink and walked out the door.

Entering the kitchen, I laid the towel on the back of my chair and slid into my chair. Aunt Mae smiled and handed me a glass of iced tea along with a napkin and a clean fork.

"Did you find the soap under the sink?" She asked. "I bought it today from the next door neighbour, and she got it from the mail lady, who had just come from making a delivery down that dirt road in the woods." Her face froze and she had that look on her face that meant that I should pay attention to what she was saying.

A loud, pounding knock came at the back door and it almost made me jump out of my skin. Aunt Mae was not startled at all, in fact, she acted like she was expecting it all the while.

"Go see who is knocking, and come back and fix your plate before everything gets cold," she said. "My back is killing me and I can't get up right now. I am tired from being bent over that stove all day."

I jumped up from the chair, and crossed to the door beside the stove, and walked out onto the back porch. I had to be careful and weave my way in and out of the large churns that were placed across the cool surface of the cement porch. The knock came one more time and I called out that I was coming.

Opening the back door, I shaded my eyes from the evening sun that was slowly setting behind the woods. There, leaning against the door, was the boy who delivered my aunt's paper to her every day. His face was pale and sweat rolled down from under his hairline and collected at the base of his sideburns.

"Here is your aunt's paper," he said in a quiet voice. "I did not feel well this morning, and waited until this evening to make my usual rounds. Please, tell your aunt that I am sorry for being so late, and that I will be glad to make it up to her next month by giving her a discount."

His eyes jerked and he lowered his head so that he would not have to look me in the face. He slid his right foot back and stepped backwards, down a step.

"Don't worry about it," I said in a reassuring voice. "She will not mind about you being a little late this evening. She has been too busy to read a newspaper anyway."

He nodded and stepped back onto the grass. I looked into his face and smiled as I began to close the door with the paper stashed under my left arm. He took a few steps and waved, before turning and walking around the corner of the house.

My body stiffened and seemed paralyzed, as I followed the boy with my eyes. Something was not quite right, and I could not figure out what it was until my eyes locked onto his hand. My stomach convulsed and a sour taste filled my mouth as tiny beads of sweat began to collect across my forehead. He was missing a finger, and his hand was wound with fresh, crisp, white, bloodstained bandages.

Originally published in Morpheus Tales #4, April 2009

Prelude By Garon Cockrell

"And for the season it was winter, and they that know the winters of that country know them to be sharp and violent, and subject to cruel and fierce storms."
William Bradford (1590 - 1657), Of Plymouth Plantation

There was a single candle burning. It was a single orange glow among a hundred dead candles, a single orange glow against the penetrating darkness inside the church.

It was once a grand cathedral filled with marble and gold. Now, the tapestry is faded, the marble has cracked, the gold long moved away. It is a shell, this church; it has not been used in years. Yet the candle still glows.

The doors and windows are sealed, boarded over. Once a colourful, warm place of worship, it has now become grey and unwelcoming. Cobwebs stretch across the pews, once red, now grey with dust. The cavernous ceiling stretches high above, its peaks lost in darkness, save for one spot. A ragged hole reveals a patch of dim sky. A single snowflake flutters through this hole. It lazily falls down, down, towards dust-covered floor. A slight gust of wind sends it spiralling towards that beacon burning in the dark. With a hiss, the snowflake burns away and the first board is yanked from the cathedral's front entrance.

The silence of the church is shattered by the loud shrill squeal of an age-old nail being pulled from its home. A moment later, a loud creek fills the air as the door is slowly pushed open. A burst of wind forces itself into the church, causing the candle to flicker violently.

"Come on then. In here." A soft voice spoke. A girl of about nine years of age stepped through the door. She was bundled into a too large winter coat, her head hidden beneath a thick hat. Behind her, an older girl entered. Her blonde hair fell to her shoulders, her ears covered by blue earmuffs, a large backpack rested on her shoulders. She turned and leaned against the door, pushing it closed.

"Shouldn't we keep going?" The younger girl asked.

"No. I can't go any further tonight. It's too cold and I am too tired."

"Will we be safe?"

The older girl shrugged.

"I don't like that answer."

"I'm sorry, Millie. I'm just so tired. I just need to rest a while." She shifted the bag from her shoulders and dropped it on the ground in front of her.

"I'm scared, Ally."

"We'll be fine. I promise." Ally detached the sleeping bag from the bottom of the pack and unrolled it, "We'll rest a while and move on. Just a little while ok?"

Millie nodded, her eyes wet with unshed tears. She pulled off her hat and a sea of dark brown curls spilled out. Ally crawled inside the sleeping bag.

"Are you tired Millie?"

Millie shook her head and looked at the door.

"We'll be fine. You keep watch for us. If you hear them coming just wake me up and we will hide."

Ally rested her head on her arm and let her eyes close slowly. She was rapidly approaching sleep when Millie spoke again.

"What was in the box?"

Ally's eyes snapped open. She stared a moment into Millie's deep brown eyes, debating.

"I... I'm not sure."

Millie turned her attention back to the door.

"It sure was big." She muttered.

"Yes," Ally whispered, "Yes it was." She lowered her head and slipped into a dream-plagued, restless sleep.

Millie stood up and glanced around the church. She was scared, but curiosity was getting the better of her. She had the need to explore. She walked down the centre aisle towards the pulpit. A memory flashed before her eyes. Millie in a white dress walking down an aisle similar to this. She smiled brightly at her parents. She could see the love in their eyes.

She was yanked back into reality at the sound of a loud crack. Almost like a firecracker.

Ally sat up quickly, all signs of sleep gone in a heartbeat.

"Millie? Millie, where are you?"

Mille ran down the aisle and crouched at Ally's side. Ally grabbed her tightly.

"Not a word." She said, her eyes locked on the door.

The noise came again, this time in rapid succession.

"Oh god." Ally whispered. She quickly climbed out of the sleeping bag and began to roll it up.

"It's them! They found us!"

"Millie, please. Grab your hat. We have to hide." But there was no time.

The door of the church was thrown open. A figure leapt inside and quickly pushed the door shut behind him.

Outside, pounding footsteps echoed in the air.

Ally grabbed Millie's hand and darted down the aisle. She could hear the person chasing after them. She could also hear the boards being yanked from the entrance.

She felt strong arms grab her from behind and pull her towards the wall. She tried to scream but a hand clamped over her mouth.

"Quiet!" The man hissed. He pushed aside a faded tapestry, and shoved Ally and Millie through the doorway behind it. He followed them through and gently lowered the cloth over the doorway seconds before the main entrance was kicked open.

Millie was paralyzed with fear. She had her arms wrapped tightly around Ally's leg. She looked at the man. In the dim light she could be see that he wasn't a man after all, but a teenage boy, his longish brown hair pulled back into a loose ponytail. He put his finger over his lips and gave Millie a wink.

Heavy footsteps filled the church quickly. Something was shouted in a language, Ally couldn't understand. Her heart was pounding in her chest. She watched as the intruder reached behind his back and pulled out a pistol.

More shouting and the footsteps retreated. The church entrance was pulled shut.

The boy lowered the gun and turned to face the girls.

"I'm sorry. I didn't know anyone would be in here."

"They... almost got us." Ally sank to her knees and began to sob.

"Look, it's okay. They didn't. You're safe."

"Why is this happening?" Ally hid her face in her hands.

Millie sat next to her and rested her head on Ally's shoulder.

"I'm Benji." He said softly. He didn't know what else to say. He sat down and leaned against the wall.

Ally looked up and wiped away her tears, "I'm Ally. This is Millie."

"Sisters?"

Ally smiled. "No. Not exactly. I found her...after the...afterwards."

"She saved me." Millie said. Her voice was veiled in a deep sadness.

Benji nodded.

"I'll go." He said.

"No. Please." Ally said, "Stay here. It's not safe out there."

Benji smiled slightly.

"I'm afraid." Ally whispered.

"Me too." Benji looked down at the ground, "It will be dark soon. We can build a fire in the other room, in the corner under the hole in the ceiling. It will be a lot colder tonight."

"You've been here before?" Millie asked.

"Yeah." Benji answered as he stood up.

"Did you light the candle?"

"Yes."

"Why?" Millie looked up at him curiously.

Benji pushed aside the tapestry. He paused and glanced towards the soft glowing candle.

"Hope, I guess. Every time I look at that candle I know I am still alive."

He stepped out of the room and let the tapestry flutter down behind him.

Through the hole in the ceiling stars shimmered dimly. A thin line of smoke threaded through the hole, invisible against the black sky.

Benji, Millie, and Ally sat around the small fire, huddled close together against the cold winter air. They nibbled at sandwiches made from food Benji had taken from a nearby store. He had it hidden in a cabinet at the front of the church.

"How long have you been here?" Ally asked.

"Two weeks."

"What happened?"

"I don't really remember. It happened so fast. All I knew to do was run."

"What about your family?"

Benji stared into the fire, his eyes glossing over.

"I'm sorry, I shouldn't have asked."

"No it's ok. My story is probably the same as yours."

"How did this happen? Why didn't anyone stop them? The army... someone?"

"I don't know. I don't know anything that is going on. I had a radio but it's just static now. I'm sure if I could find a TV that worked it would be the same thing. That is, if there was power anymore. From what I can tell from the radio is that they attacked at the same time from all directions. People said they were speaking Russian and Chinese. They came in and killed without mercy. Killed my mother and my father. I watched them put a gun to my little brother's head. I've never seen such hatred in my life. I don't understand it. I can't fathom it. But, there it was right in front of my face. They didn't see me at first. My father did. He was crying. His eyes locked with mine, and in my head I heard his voice. Clearer than anything I have ever heard before. He told me to run."

Ally wiped her eyes.

"My daddy fought with them." Millie said softly, "The bad men came and he fought them. But they shot him and he is dead now. I ran with my brother but they got him too, and I was by myself until Ally found me."

"Where do we go from here?" Ally asked.

"There's no where left to go. There's nothing left. It's gone."

"What do you mean?"

But Benji did not answer. He tossed the last of his sandwich into the fire.

"I don't know why there was no one to stop them." He said, "I don't know why any of this is happening."

"It wasn't soldiers who killed my family." Ally whispered. "They came to our town. We saw them killing people and...they were doing other things to the women. My dad...he had these pills. I don't know where he got them or why he even had them. He was always paranoid about that sort of thing. It drove my mom nuts. He always looked at these conspiracy sites and all that. But... anyway.

When he saw them... When he saw what they were doing... He begged us to take this pill. He took it, and my mom, and older sister and her kids took it. I...I didn't. I was too scared. Scared more of dying than facing these monsters. I watched them all die and then I ran. I was alone for awhile. Scared to death. A few times I wanted to just give myself to them and let it all end. What was the point? Everywhere I looked I saw death and destruction. I found Millie just outside of the city. She was standing in the middle of the road staring a butterfly. She had a smile on her face. Behind her a building was burning, sending this thick black smoke into the air, and there she was smiling at a butterfly. She became my reason to keep going."

"And here you are." Benji said.

"Here we are."

Benji stood and walked towards his burning candle.

"I'm sleepy, Ally." Millie said.

"Ok. Here, climb in the sleeping bag." Ally helped her climb in the bag, "The fire will keep you warm."

Ally rubbed Millie's hair as she fell asleep. A look of peace crossed her face, a slight smile danced across her mouth. Ally kissed her forehead and stood up. She walked to where Benji stood.

"Are you ok?"

"Not really."

"We'll be ok."

Benji was silent. He ran his finger over the flame.

"I don't think so." Benji sighed.

"Why not? We can pack up and leave in the morning. We can be out of the city by noon."

"There's nowhere to go."

"We'll find other people Benji. We'll start over. Those soldiers can't stay here forever."

"You don't understand."

"We can start over somewhere else. Somewhere they've left. We'll find more survivors."

"There are no more survivors!" Benji shouted. "There is nowhere left for us to go."

"What are you saying?"

"They've destroyed it all. America is dead, Ally. It's gone. Wiped away. Dust. Poof." Benji picked up his candle and blew it out, "There is no more hope."

Benji brushed past her and pulled open the church door. He walked outside and disappeared into the night.

Ally didn't want to think about what he said. She didn't believe it was true. There was always hope. She realized that when she found Millie.

There is always hope.

Benji stood in the shadows across the street from the church. He felt bad for shouting at Ally, but his fears and frustrations got the better of him. He saw the soldiers carrying the box off the truck. He knew what was inside of it. He knew what was coming. He just didn't now how to escape it.

When he came back inside the church he noticed his candle was lit again. Beside it, two more candles burned brightly. Benji watched the flickering light for a few moments before he lay down next to the dwindling fire and fell into a deep sleep.

In the morning, they woke to find three soldiers standing above them. Millie instantly began to cry. Ally grabbed her and pulled her to her chest.

"Get Up!" One spoke, barely understandable through his Russian accent.

Benji looked desperately for his gun.

He shouted again. "GET UP!"

The three of them stood up slowly.

"Please don't hurt us." Ally pleaded.

"Be quiet bitch!"

"They're going to kill us." Benji said, "We have to run."

The lead soldier cocked his head slightly. He was listening to the radio in his ear. He turned to his peers and waved them out the door. He turned back to them and grinned. Then lowered his weapon.

"Perhaps you prefer the bullet no?" He said in his thick Russian accent. He laughed and ran out of the church.

"Benji what's happening? Where are they going?"

"We have to go. Now."

Above them the sound of helicopters filled the air.

"What's going on?" Ally said as she grabbed her bag.

"They're leaving."

"Leaving? Then we're safe? They're going! Why are we running?"

Benji turned to her. He placed his hands on her shoulders and looked into her eyes.

"We have to run Ally." He said more to her with his eyes.

"Oh no... " She whispered.

"We have to go now."

Millie grabbed Ally's hand and in turn Ally grabbed Benji's. Together they ran out of the church.

In the sky, dozens of helicopters roared overhead as they ran. They ran past the crumbling buildings and the burning cars. The sun was a bright beacon in the sky. They ran and they ran. Millie tripped and Ally scooped her up into her arms. Millie watched behind them as they ran. Her chin was resting on Ally's shoulder.

"Ally... " She said with a laugh in her voice, "Another sun!"

"Don't look, baby. Close your eyes."

Benji looked at her and squeezed her hand tighter.

###

"Hope." He said to her. They ran faster.

The ground shook.

"Benji... " Ally whispered.

In the church, the three burning candles flared impossibly bright before succumbing to the coming monster. And as they ran, the last burning ray of hope warming their hearts; Ally, Benji, and Millie's world ceased and the darkness overtook them.

Originally published in Morpheus Tales #4, April 2009

The Salty Skeleton By Theresa C. Newbill

A hand forged pony shoe digs out of the ground on an old logging trail in the woods of Decatur, Alabama. A black man and a white woman dance horizontally among arrant spices of herb bushes and scented vines, setting a small part of the pantomime. They are oblivious to the shrouded figures heading their way. Ten men wear the breeches of white masks. The patriarch of the group grabs the woman. She looks up and catches her breath. He takes out a hunting knife, cuts at her eyes and slices at her mouth while calling her a nigger lover. The laughter of evil is heard through the fierce recanting screams between the sobs. Each takes their turn beating, spitting, cutting, penetrating her more deeply than any words. The leaves are shaken as sun bleached stones are heard hitting the black man's flesh with fatal magnitude. Blood flows over the edges of earth into the crevices of leaves. Silence lies on silence.

###

Elsa May Smith sucks on some sweet berries that have ripened in the wilderness. Her lilac perfume hangs in the ecstatic air, a paranormal souvenir of her daily visits. The battering of voodoo drums is heard from the nearby house as the day creeps down into night. Blood crosses smear the trunks of trees and a cock crows.

"The spirits live as you live." Clothed from head to toe in white apparel, Mamma Della emerges with cigar in hand. A barking dog at her side also announces its presence. Elsa May exhibits a bold grin on her face. "I brought you something, child." Mamma Della makes a motion with her wrist, turning the object in her hand three times counter clockwise as she inhales and exhales manic puffs of smoke from her cigar. The mutt lies down quietly by her side. "This belonged to my grandmother who passed it down to me, and now it's yours, three times blessed." Elsa May holds the pendant in her hands. "It's so beautiful!" Mamma Della licks her fingers and puts out the cigar. "It's made of Dendritic Quartz. It will bring the energy of the stars into your soul, heal you when you are sick, and heighten your consciousness. It will protect you from all harm. Take it child! Wear it too." Elsa May graciously accepts. Mamma Della holds Elsa May's face in her hands that show all too well her fifty years on this Earth. "Words that come out of us, like words from within, tie us to those we love, forever."

They begin to walk. A storm is brewing through the crying of winds, which has the mutt spooked. He takes off in a sprint ahead of them. Mamma Della laughs and looks up at the sky, "The physical world is meaningless tonight." As they approach Mamma Della's house, music from a radio plays. An old woman sits on a porch swing, the tiny sized radio at her side. She fiddles with the tuning and antenna, feeling her way with her fingers. Deep scars are displayed across her face, eyes and mouth. "How is your mother doing?" Elsa May asks. Mamma Della sighs as she looks at the aged woman on the porch swing. "Dying of diabetes, dear one."

The interior corridor of the house holds a representation of Baron Samedi - The Loa of the Dead. He is wearing a top hat, black coat tails, sunglasses, and is smoking a cigar. An altar is erected in his honour with various candles, symbols, colourful beads, bells, samhain oil, and rum. Mamma Della's son, Marcos, plays the voodoo drums. Elsa May gives him a knowing nod, and Marcos responds with a flirtatious smile, still tapping the rhythm out on the drum.

"How far along are you?" A raspy almost unintelligible voice from behind them surfaces. It is Mamma Della's mother. Elsa May turns around and puts her hands on her stomach. "Three months." She looks back at Marcos who is in a trance still tapping on the drum. Mamma Della turns to Elsa May. "Are you ready to do this, child?" Elsa May agrees and with that they walk up the spiral staircase into a scrying room. The room is painted completely black and is empty except for a chair carefully placed in front of a large oval mirror. Mamma Della instructs Elsa May to sit. "Clear your mind and your heart; be open to the forces that will guide you." Mamma Della's mother brings an herbal drink and hands it to Elsa May. "Drink now." She says. Elsa May drinks and starts to feel her head spinning. She is nauseous. Trying to keep herself from passing out, she focuses her eyes on the mirror. She dreams a little and feels the dark. Images start to appear in the mirror, and then voices. Like a film playing.

A black man and a white woman dance horizontally among arrant spices of herb bushes and scented vines... "Nigger lover!" Elsa May's eyes widen and she whispers "Grandfather? No!" A white woman is being violently assaulted. A black man is tied to a tree. "If we let this nigger go, it won't be safe for your mother, wife, or sweetheart to walk down the streets of the South!" Each of the men takes their turn stoning the black man to death. "I can't see his body." Elsa May says. "The body is no body to be seen." Mamma Della responds. "It is from the Earth he came and it is the Earth that will fate him back to us by the power of Ghede. My love, my husband." Mamma Della's mother says. Elsa May stands not noticing Marcos in the doorway, the sounds of the voodoo drums, silent. "Reincarnation. His! How is that possible?" Elsa May asks. Mamma Della moves in close to Elsa May, and places her hand on the girl's stomach. Marcos grins as Elsa May looks on in horror. The bareness of the house is filled with the breeding and bearing birth of harmony. And retribution.

Originally published in Morpheus Tales #4, April 2009

A Story About Monsters By Adrian Ludens

The bad thing was going to happen again. I could hear my stepfather's footsteps approaching from the hall. Then my bedroom door opened and he was briefly silhouetted in the light. He closed the door behind him and darkness filled the room. I heard the dull thump of his whiskey bottle when he set it on my dresser, then the floorboards creaked as he moved toward me.

I lay still.

I told myself I was sleeping.

I was in a coma.

I was dead.

I could hear my stepfather breathing now, almost panting. The starlight that crept through my window was enough for me to see that his hands were moving. One of them was, anyway.

Then my stepfather froze. He looked down at his feet and noticed the sinewy, snakelike tendrils that looped around his ankles.

The monster that lived under my bed yanked with such strength that my stepfather was a blur as he flew to the floor. His head made a loud crack on the hardwood and I was barely able to make out the whites of his terrified eyes before he was completely dragged under my bed. The crunching of bones mixed with wet sucking sounds came next.

I was so focused on what was going on under my bed that I didn't hear my mama approaching. She threw open my bedroom door and stood there with her hands on her hips.

"She givin' you trouble Roy?" Mama's voice was shrill. She flipped on the overhead light to survey the situation.

"I heard a noise," she said to me. "Where's Roy?"

"He was goin' to hurt me again," I began, trying to explain. Mama's face grew ashen, then anger blossomed on her gaunt cheeks.

"What have you done to my Roy?"

"Nothin' Mama, I swear!"

"Then where is he? If you've hurt him... "

Mama stopped talking and gaped, horrified, at the floor beside my bed. I peeped over the edge of the mattress. There was dark red liquid pooling out from underneath.

"You uppity little pinhead! You should be thankful for the attention!" She spun around and went to my dresser.

I don't know why, but the way my mama was acting reminded me of the day I heard my teacher, Mrs. Amos, telling another lady that my mama was not right in the head. Even though I heard her say it, I didn't argue with her 'cause I figured she was right.

"I'm gonna make you pay dearly for hurtin' him," Mama growled. She grabbed the half-empty whiskey bottle and threw it at me. I ducked and the bottle shattered on the wall, spraying everything. What a mess!

My bed sheets smelled like stinky rubbing alcohol, and I wrinkled my nose as I started to crawl out of bed. I knew I'd have to be careful and go slow to avoid the pieces of broken glass. I didn't want to get all cut up. Mama fished around in her bathrobe, and before I got very far I saw her hold up her lighter in triumph. All of a sudden, I got real scared.

"Oh Mama, no!" I cried. "Please, please, please Mama no!" I tried not to sound like a whiny baby but it was really hard. Mama's eyes had a funny glint in them; like she was happy and mad and scared and sad all at the same time. I couldn't look away from those eyes so I just sat there like I was froze.

My closet door flew open so hard it busted right off the hinges and something dark hurtled from inside. It landed on Mama's back and they both went sprawling. The monster that lived in my closet looked like a big ball of dirty, matted black fur. I thought the top half of its body was going to tip over backwards from the rest of it, but then I realized the monster was just opening its mouth. I looked away and counted glass shards in my covers for a while. When I looked up again, it was too soon. I saw the monster sitting on my floor, munching away. Sticking out of its mouth was my mama's hand, still clutching her lighter.

Then the light started to fade and everything got really dim, really quick. All I saw was black and I don't remember what happened next.

#

I was eating dry cereal and cautiously looking around for Mama and Roy when the policeman knocked on the door the next morning. He said there had been reports of a disturbance.

I told him that my mama had been hollering at me and was fixing to start me on fire last night but that she wasn't in the house anymore. I guess I didn't lie.

The policeman didn't look very happy and he asked me to show him where it happened. We went upstairs to my bedroom and there was the lighter on the floor and the broken glass on the bed. The policeman smelled my bed sheets and looked even less happy. He hustled me out of the room but one thing I noticed before he got me out of there was that the blood on my floor was all gone. The monster under my bed liked Roy enough to lick the plate, I guess.

Some people came to take me away.

Nobody saw Mama or my stepfather ever again. They sure looked for them, though.

Finally, I got sent to live in a new house with a new family. It is very nice here. I get to eat lots of good food and they have a puppy who loves to play with me. Plus, my new mama and dad never yell at me or try to start me on fire or hurt me down there. My new mama is named Carole, but I call her Mama Foster because I heard lots of people call her my Foster Mother. My new daddy - whose real name is Neal, but who I call Daddy Foster- always tells me bedtime stories. Sometimes he tells silly stories about monsters hiding under my bed or in my closet and I just laugh.

There aren't any monsters living in my room. Good monsters only live with kids who need protecting. And in this house, there aren't any bad monsters who sleep just down the hall.

Originally published in Morpheus Tales #4, April 2009

Epitaph For Sol By Tommy B. Smith

As the wrath of Heaven's might seemed flung down upon them, it was with blind panic and remorseful agony that the inhabitants of Sol were swept up in the Dance of Death. Wild and raving were those afflicted, extremities burning and bodies covered in parasites driven of divine judgment, microscopic beasts with a hunger so determined that every blemish of purity became a morsel of rapt delicacy.

Those caught in the harshest rigors of the holy torment were burned throughout by an inner fire, its intensity so great that it might have consumed their souls during the final moments. Those with the luxury of a quick means to die launched themselves from the highest windows to the compassion of the ground far below. Death was the salvation of Sol, and for those who would live, peace of mind would remain ever the fleeting illusion.

The New Faith came to Sol, its zealots baptized in the fire of its wicked absurdities. In answer, the crimson dragon of righteousness descended to devour what remained of the condemned village.

The town's only place of worship burned, dispensed to its grim sentence by those who writhed in the torturous madness of the searing heavenly light. They had lost their will to the demons, and revelled in the destruction of this renounced spiritual icon.

Father Hamund watched it burn. Even as he clung to his faith, and to his belief that mankind could defy its own monstrosity through the boundless guidance of the written word, the fires were reflected in his sombre eyes. His face was weary, lined with age and grief. Sol was destroying itself. Sol wanted to die.

So quickly after the village's yearly Festival of Grace, the demons had come to Sol. They had named their favourites. The rest had been devoured as the demons began their wicked feast and dined on those who lacked the strength to defy the yawning nether regions of their appetites.

For the wives who were with child, a horrific spell was unleashed, and they were pushed into the pains of immediate childbirth. The forced offspring, thought a product of the blackest phantoms, were gathered by those either taken by demonic influence or consumed by holy vengeance. Father Hamund dared not contemplate their fates.

Gontier, one of the village elders, claimed his seat as the harbinger of the New Faith. As prime subject of the forces that governed the undoing of Sol, Gontier directed his maniacal enthusiasts to burn the holy place, and committed himself to the eradication of the enduring righteous.

Father Hamund had the protection of his faith, and he had not been touched. He watched the flames engulf every ember of the simple structure that was Sol's lone cathedral, until his veil of sadness was pierced by the scream from across the main square.

"Leave me be!" a child wailed as he was dragged toward the blazing cathedral. Two men of the New Faith pulled him along, one by each arm, under the supervision of Gontier. They laughed at his vain struggles.

"Into the glare!" the men shouted in gleeful unison. "Into the glare! Into the glare!" The horrified child screeched in terror. He struggled and pleaded, but his captors continued to drag him toward the impending flames.

"No!" he screamed as they lifted him from his feet and prepared to hurl him into the fire.

"Unhand the boy!" Father Hamund roared. He charged forward. The men received his rapid advance with eyes glazed from the madness. Gontier crossed his arms and looked to Father Hamund with a smug half-smile. His demeanour scarcely masked his growing excitement.

"He received the boy with great happiness," Gontier spoke in an authoritative tone, as though reciting a widely recognized passage in some perversion of a religious service. "And His will was then fed by a speaker of divine falsehoods, and this brought Him and His beloved everlasting joy!"

Father Hamund threw himself forward, and his body connected with one of the men. The action came a moment too late. The boy was hurled forward at the same instant.

The boy landed just outside of the fire's reach. The heat singed his flesh as he stumbled, and Hamund's heart skipped a beat. While the man who had been struck by the priest was knocked to the ground in surprise, the other man pulled a knife from his belt.

Father Hamund lunged toward the fire. He seized the boy's wrist and yanked him backward to safety in time, but as he did so, he was unaware of Gontier's armed accomplice advancing toward him from behind. The boy cried out a warning. Father Hamund turned, and the knife was thrust forth.

Father Hamund gasped as the blade gashed his shoulder. The two men grappled, and Father Hamund twisted the knife from his attacker's grip. With his assailant disarmed, he backed away. Blood soaked the clothing near his wound. While it was not a critical injury, the pain in his shoulder was sharp.

Gontier babbled with insistence that the men should kill both Father Hamund and the boy without hesitation. Father Hamund threw his uninjured arm around the boy and hauled him away from the scene faster than the child's small legs could carry him.

As someone heaved and vomited nearby while another spasmed uncontrollably on the ground, Father Hamund looked one last time to the dying cathedral. His eyes spoke a silent farewell.

In Sol, there was no one left to save. Drawing the young boy along with him, Hamund turned and fled the doomed village.

It was night when the two slowed their trek from Sol. The panic still haunted the boy's eyes, but it was obvious that fatigue now dulled his senses. Father Hamund attempted to make conversation, if only to keep the boy alert to continue their retreat.

"What is your name?"

The boy flinched at the sudden question. He swallowed and said nothing for a time, but then turned his face to Hamund. His countenance was ashen and etched with sorrow.

"Arnaud," the boy replied. Father Hamund could hear the reluctance in his quiet voice, and did not press him further. The boy had seen far too much pain for one so young.

"I will see to it that you are safe," Hamund spoke. Nothing else was said for the remainder of the journey into the night, until the two made a stop to rest and took a meal. Father Hamund, though nagged by an unshakable paranoia, deduced the likelihood that Gontier had not pursued them in their journey, nor had any of the others who were seized by the infernal persuasions of the New Faith.

Father Hamund produced the bread and cheese from his pack and offered the larger portion to the boy, who was thin and from an apparent impoverished upbringing. The boy thanked Father Hamund, but declined.

After several more fruitless attempts to share his fare with young Arnaud, Father Hamund ate alone. It was a light meal, but the cheese and rye bread would keep his hunger away for now.

It was an undeterminable span of time, later into the night, during the darkest hours, when Father Hamund began to feel the Devil's madness creep into him. He felt the fire begin to overtake him, and his grip on reality began to slacken.

He spent the late hour in prayer, but with every sincere word uttered, the fire only seemed to grow in its insistence.

He looked to Arnaud, who lay in peaceful slumber a distance away. Father Hamund took into his hands the knife he had wrested from one of Gontier's men in Sol, the one who had wounded him.

The fire now burned him with unrelenting vigilance, and Father Hamund realized that he would soon be taken by the same demonic influence that had razed the cathedral, and had swallowed the rest of Sol into nothingness. He looked again to Arnaud, and realized that the young one would soon be prey to these demons that had meant once before to bring his youthful, innocent few years to an end. Father Hamund was losing himself to the demons' terrible whims, and once this was done, the boy's well-being, both physical and spiritual, would be at risk.

Questions of salvation weighed on Father Hamund's ailing mind as he turned the knife over in his wrinkled hands. A tear spilled down his cheek. He looked up to the starry heavens, and pressed the knife against his wrist.

"Father, please forgive me for what I must do," he whispered.

#

In the Middle Ages, the affliction known in history as Saint Anthony's Fire raged periodically through Europe. By the year 1676, a scientific discovery by Denis Dodart revealed that the nature of Saint Anthony's Fire, also known as the Holy Fire, was a product of ergot poisoning due to the consumption of contaminated rye bread. It is speculated that this phenomenon may have also been responsible for the hysteria that manifested in Salem, Massachusetts in 1692.

Originally published in Morpheus Tales #4, April 2009